My name is Winter Frey.
My friend Cal was a hunted fugitive.
Our story continues . . .

CONSPIRACY 365

MALICE

To Elizabeth Nicole Butler

First American Paperback Edition
First American Edition 2013
Kane Miller, A Division of EDC Publishing

First published by Scholastic Australia Pty Limited in 2012
This edition published under license from Scholastic Australia Pty Limited.

For information contact:
Kane Miller, A Division of EDC Publishing
PO Box 470663
Tulsa, OK 74147-0663
www.kanemiller.com
www.edcpub.com
www.usbornebooksandmore.com

Library of Congress Control Number: 2012952000

Printed and bound in the United States of America
1 2 3 4 5 6 7 8 9 10
ISBN: 978-1-61067-219-1

CONSPIRACY 365

MALICE

GABRIELLE LORD

Kane Miller
A DIVISION OF EDC PUBLISHING

Prologue

I skidded my motorbike to a halt outside Winter's house. The place looked great now that it had been painted a really cool blue and the garden was full of plants and trees. But I wasn't in the mood to appreciate it. Winter had called me earlier, her voice agitated.

"Something really weird came in the mail today," she'd said. "And Cal, there've been other things too."

I didn't like the sound of that at all and had stopped packing for my trip to flight school. I couldn't quite believe that I'd managed to score a place on a prestigious pilot training program and I'd been thinking of little else for weeks now. Although I had noticed Winter hadn't been her usual self for the past couple of days. Had I been neglecting Winter? I'd grabbed my keys and headed out the door.

Things had been awesome for all of us in recent months. Mum seemed happier than she had been in ages and Gabbi was doing well in school. And as for my friends, we'd never been closer after all we'd been through—the huge and dangerous quest to discover the truth about the Ormond Singularity, the bomb at City Hall and then the final showdown with Sligo and Elijah on the Sapphire Star cruise ship. Now that all that was behind me, I had a real chance to achieve my dream, to become a real pilot . . . just like Dad and I had always talked about.

But there was no time for those thoughts now, as I arrived at Winter's house. I pulled off my helmet, used my key to get in, and ran upstairs to the study where I could hear voices.

Winter and Boges barely greeted me, completely engrossed with what looked like an ordinary stamped envelope.

"You said something came in the mail," I said. "Is that it?"

"It's what's inside that's worrying me," said Boges, his face serious. "Take a look."

I took the envelope and opened it, frowning because for a minute I thought it was empty. Then I saw a scrap of torn newspaper, which I lifted out carefully. My thoughts immediately flicked to the vicious articles that reporter Ben Willoughby had written about me long ago, before we became almost friends. I wondered if he was up to his old tricks again.

But I quickly realized this didn't look like his handiwork. It looked like the top right corner of a very old newspaper. There were four words— two in thick black print, and another two, added like an afterthought, in scrawling handwriting.

As I read them, a chill crept up my spine.

DAY 1

30 days to go . . .

Home
Mansfield Way, Dolphin Point

6:25 pm

Cal looked at me, frowning.

"What does it mean?" he asked, his blue eyes narrowed in concern.

"I haven't got a clue," I said.

He stared at the words again.

"On the phone, you mentioned . . . other things," he said after a long pause. I knew he'd noticed how I'd been over the last few days—edgy and anxious, answering his worried questions with my standard response—*stop questioning me, everything is fine*. Now it was time to come clean.

"Someone's been here," I said. "In my place."

"When? Who?"

"I don't know who—or when. And it wasn't just once. I think it started a few days ago. At first, I thought I was just imagining it. I noticed things being in a slightly different place than where I'd left them."

"How do you know someone's been here with all this . . . " Boges opened his arms to take in the mess of paper files and documents that covered most of the desk, spilling over onto the sofa and chairs in my study ". . . this *stuff* piled up everywhere?"

"I live alone, Boges," I explained defensively, "no one comes up here but me. And I wasn't expecting guests in my study!"

I walked around, nervously picking up a photograph of my parents, putting it down again and adjusting the position of the potted plant that stood nearby. "Look, I did think I was going nuts or something. Because nothing was moved very much. Like my diary—*especially* my diary. Then I found this on the floor near my desk." I showed them the scrunched-up bit of blue, yellow and white paper. "It's a chewing gum wrapper— Triple Mint. I don't chew gum. So I definitely didn't drop this here."

"Is that your diary?" Boges asked. "That red and gold book?"

"Yes," I said, nodding, "I'm a bit particular and I always put my diary like this, between the wood joints in my desk." My desk was made of recycled wood, just like floorboards. Cal and Boges watched as I placed the diary next to the computer between two of the boards, straightening it until the top and bottom edges fitted exactly between the joints. "Twice now, it hasn't been in the right place."

"You could've bumped it when you were getting up from your desk," Boges suggested.

"I thought of that," I said, picking it up, opening it. "But whenever I finish writing up an entry, I always use this bookmark." I touched the dark-red ribbon attached to the spine of the diary. "I mark the following day's page, so that it's ready for me to open. But look—" I said, passing the diary to Cal, "it's been left in this page."

"That's from two days ago," he said.

"Right . . . which means someone has been reading my diary."

Cal scanned my handwritten entry for the day, reading it out loud—

THURSDAY

More boring work filling out forms to transfer property deeds from Sligo's name to mine. Reminder—must check with lawyer when to bring them in for witnessing and signing. Perdita computer file empty. I'll search for paper file and then I guess I'll have to copy it in. I'd much rather be at the movies.

"It's just me complaining about the paperwork I have to do," I explained. "Some documents only exist in paper files because my father hadn't gotten around to entering all of them into the database. Sligo had other things on his mind instead of keeping up with paperwork, so I've been going through the files and making sure that they're all in order."

"There doesn't seem to be anything particularly earth-shattering in that entry," Cal said.

"When I realized my diary was open on that page this morning, I went looking for the Perdita file and spotted it right at the bottom of this pile," I said, picking up the folder from my desk.

"Perdita. Unusual name . . . I wonder who it is."

"I don't know," I said. "The name is pretty cool though. It's the name of the heroine from Shakespeare's *The Winter's Tale*. And Perdita means 'the lost one.' I used to feel like that."

Cal nodded—he knew what I meant.

I opened the file and started flicking through some papers, the boys looking over my shoulder. "I'm not sure what this is . . . 'notice of easement', some legal letters . . . " I said. "I'd better spend some time going through this carefully to find out what this has to do with someone called Perdita." I put the file back on top of the pile.

"OK," I continued, picking up the torn piece of newspaper again. "What are we supposed to make of this? Who's the Drowner?" I asked. "Why did someone write '30 days'? And why have they sent this to *me*? Is it a threat?"

"It's from some really old newspaper," Cal said, noticing the date. "Nineteen sixty two. Half a century ago. Looks like the last part of the headline has been torn off and then someone's just scrawled '30 days' after it."

Boges took the scrap of yellowing newspaper from my fingers and had a closer look. "Thirty days from now . . . does that date ring any bells?"

It didn't mean anything to me and I could see from the faces of the others that they'd all drawn a blank.

"I hope it isn't a repeat of what happened before. Elijah is locked up, isn't he? I mean, the last time we got a note like this, we nearly got blown up!" Cal said. I could see he was trying to be light-hearted, but I knew the confrontation with Sligo on the Sapphire Star still bothered him.

"The Drowner sounds more like some murderer or gangster . . . or a serial killer," Boges continued, pulling out his phone.

"Great," I said bitterly. "Just what a girl needs. A serial killer. With a thing for old newspaper clippings."

"Take it easy. I'm checking it right now," Boges announced, hovering over his phone.

"Well?" I asked. A few moments later, Boges was shaking his head. "The only thing I can find called *The Drowner* is a book, and it wasn't around in 1962. And don't worry, Cal, your pathological cousin is still in detention as far as I can tell."

"Repro might know. I'll give him a call," Cal said, reaching for his phone. He left a message asking his old friend to call back. "Repro's gone a bit funny about cell phones," Cal said. "Ever since he read that they have GPS tracking in them, he keeps his in a locked metal box."

"That won't help," laughed Boges. "I hope he gets it out every now and then to listen to his messages."

"So what can the note mean?" I asked. "And who would have sent it?"

My questions hung in the air like accusations. Then I was struck by a frightening thought. "What if Sligo wasn't the only one who got out of Inisrue Marsh?"

"Come on, Winter. That's not very likely," said Boges.

I took a closer look at the envelope and then turned the piece of newspaper over. The faded print on the back seemed to be a list of vegetable prices at a local market. Nothing helpful there. "If one person got out, Boges, it's possible that someone else did too," I reminded him.

"Perhaps we should call the police," Cal said, "if you really believe someone has been in here."

"Yes, but how could I prove it? By saying my diary is on a different page? They're not going to take that seriously. And what could they do about it anyway? Can you imagine what Senior Sergeant McGrath would say?" I said.

Boges cocked his head to one side, and his eyebrows came together like they always do when he's thinking hard.

"What is it, Boges?" Cal asked. "You've got an idea. Spit it out."

"Looks to me like we've got two problems. First of all, there's this newspaper clipping, and second, someone's been stalking Winter. We can solve the second problem quite quickly. If someone's been snooping around in here, there's a really easy way to find out who it is. Once we've cleared that up, we can start tracking down the Drowner—whoever he is."

Cal's House
Flood Street, Richmond

7:40 pm

Boges headed off, promising to come back the next day to solve the stalker mystery, while Cal and

I went to his place. Cal knew his mum would be happy to have me stay in the guest room. I would have been fine at my place, but Cal insisted.

I followed Cal up to his room where piles of gear took up most of the flat surfaces. I picked up his new pilot's bag.

"Dad promised me he'd buy me a real pilot's bag when I got my solo flying rating, but by the time I did that, he wasn't around anymore. I figured I'd go ahead and get myself one."

So much had happened since Cal's father had died, but Cal still missed him just as badly as ever.

"What is all this stuff?" I asked, pulling out his headset and fiddling with a slide rule. "Is this for navigation?"

Cal gently took the slide rule out of my hands and put it back in the bag. "Why didn't you tell me when you first noticed someone had been sniffing around?" he asked. "Why leave it till now, when I'm about to go away for three weeks?"

"I didn't want you to be worried while you were away."

"Don't ever do that again. OK? If something happens that bothers you, tell me right away." He took my hands in his, holding them tight. "Winter, listen to me. I've gotta go, but if anything happens or if you get really scared, promise me you'll call?"

"Cal, I'm going to be all right. And I've got Boges and Ryan. Don't worry. You need to focus on this. I know how hard it was to get into the course."

"Promise me?"

I wasn't one hundred percent sure about keeping this promise, but I gave in. "Promise," I said, hugging him.

"I'll call Ryan now," Cal said. "You can tell him what's going on."

"I've got a better idea," I said, feeling a big smile on my face. "How about all of us get together at my place tomorrow night for dinner? We can celebrate the fact that I'm almost through that mountain of paperwork. What do you say?"

"I say yes," Cal said.

DAY 2

29 days to go . . .

Home
Mansfield Way, Dolphin Point

9:15 pm

The next night, we all sat around my big dining table after a fantastic meal. I'd twisted up my hair into a knot, and put on a pair of long sparkling earrings. My spirits were sparkling too. I felt better having shared my worries with my friends and I knew we'd get to the bottom of these mysteries.

I hadn't seen Ryan for a while. He was wearing black jeans and a black band T-shirt and he'd styled his hair up into spikes. It was amazing how similar Cal and Ryan were—they had the same tastes in music and food . . . but not in clothes! Cal was so lucky to have found a brother he got along so well with—most of the time.

Boges excused himself and went upstairs as I told Ryan about the suspicious chewing gum wrapper and how I'd been spooked by *The Drowner* note.

When we realized Boges hadn't come back, we went upstairs and found him in my study, standing on a chair which was precariously balanced on top of my desk. He was fiddling with the light in the ceiling. I grabbed the legs of the chair to make sure he didn't fall.

"Just fitting this little spy camera up here," Boges said, looking down at us and almost losing his balance. "No one will notice it. I've patched it into the electrical wiring."

"That sounds dangerous," Cal said.

"Only if it kills you, dude. How does that look?" He took his hand away and I looked at the ceiling light. I couldn't see anything at first.

"Is that it?" I asked, pointing to a tiny, round black object just inside the silver rim of the light housing.

"That's it," said Boges, climbing down from the chair onto the desk and then thudding heavily onto the floor.

"Cool," said Ryan. "There's no way anyone would notice it. You'd really have to get close-up. Even then it just looks like the head of a small rivet or something."

"All I have to do now," said Boges, as we all crowded around his laptop, "is activate it." He pushed a couple of buttons. "That's odd," he said, as he stared at the screen. "I've only just switched it on, I haven't even activated it yet, but I'm picking up some kind of interference . . ." Again, his voice trailed off and he looked up, his eyebrows colliding with concern. "This isn't right. There is something seriously weird going on here." He looked around. He was starting to seem really worried.

"What is it, Boges?" I said. "You're freaking me out."

"Tell us," Cal demanded, looking at a small signal pulsing like a heartbeat on Boges's screen. "What's seriously weird?"

"Apart from you, Boges," Ryan tried to joke. But no one laughed.

Boges typed in some commands and on cue, his screen immediately filled. The camera was activated and there we were, or rather a bird's-eye view of us, all grouped around my desk.

"There's nothing wrong with that," Cal said, pointing to us all on the screen and waving to himself.

"It's not my camera I'm worried about. It's something else. Switch off your phones, will you? All of you."

We did as he asked and a few moments later, Boges shook his head. "It's not your phones either. I'm picking up interference that shouldn't be here, right at the end of the FM band."

"So what does that mean?" Ryan asked.

"Boges, explain!" I demanded.

Boges thought for a moment, then said, "It means there's some other activity going on here."

There followed a long pause until Cal looked across at me as comprehension dawned. Ryan got it too.

"You've picked up another signal," I said, "haven't you? Something was already here and it showed up on your screen."

"Winter," said Boges gravely, "this is bad news. Someone's bugged your study."

For a few seconds, none of us could move or speak. Intruders who chewed gum, threatening newspaper clippings and now someone bugging my house. I couldn't believe it. *What was going on?*

"We already know that someone's gotten into your place and searched around," Boges continued. "But it looks like they've also planted a bug, or you've brought something into your study that's hiding it."

"Like what?" I asked.

"Could be anything—a clock, radio, lamp, calculator, a pen . . . "

"No. I haven't got anything new . . . " Then I remembered something. "There was a free gift that came with a catalog I got last week. It's here somewhere. It's a really neat pen . . . there it is, next to the pile of folders. Hey, what are you doing, Boges?"

Instead of picking up the pen, Boges had swung around, grabbed my little radio from the bookshelf, tuned it to FM, switched it to Mono and turned up the volume. An unearthly squeal filled the room as he approached the desk where the pen lay.

"What *is* that?" Ryan yelled.

"Commonly called a 'squealer'," said Boges. "Otherwise known as feedback detection, or loop detection. Watch this." As he moved the FM radio closer to the black pen on my desk, the squealing sound became more high-pitched.

"That pen?" I asked, incredulous.

Boges nodded, bringing the little radio right in close to the pen. The squealing became unbearable in pitch. "That's your bug. Take a closer look."

I lifted the pen off the desk. It seemed like a normal pen with a screw-off cap . . . until I looked really closely. "Boges! Turn that radio down. It's deafening!"

"Sorry!" Boges grimaced. "But take a look at the top of the cap."

"It's tiny! It's like a little bead. It's even

smaller than the one I wore around my neck at Sligo's dinner! I can't believe it! It's been sitting right here on my desk, watching everything I did. That means they've seen you installing your camera, Boges. The whole thing's been a waste of time. They know we're on to them!"

"I don't think so," Boges said. "This kind of bug looks like an audio transmitter. I doubt it's got the capacity to do visual surveillance as well. In any case, I'm going to check every room now." Boges took the radio and his laptop with him. As he left, the squealing sound faded.

9:44 pm

We waited, looking from one to the other nervously. Boges finally came back, shaking his head. "I'm not picking up anything anywhere else in the house. So it's just this bug in your study."

I looked around wildly. "Why? Why on earth is someone spying on *me*? I don't have anything that valuable, and anyway, why didn't they just steal whatever it is they wanted when they were in here?"

Ryan jumped off the desk that he'd been sitting on, his face lit up. "That means it must be something that's not obvious. Something they couldn't find."

"Makes sense, dude," said Boges, warming to

the idea. "But that doesn't narrow it down enough."

"Hang on," Cal said, "maybe it's a document that they're after, you know, some valuable share certificate or bank document or something. Could be something in this huge pile."

I went to check the stack on the right-hand side of the computer and I suddenly stopped in my tracks. "Look! The Perdita folder . . . it's gone! It was just sitting there on the top of the pile. You saw me put it there yesterday after I'd found it at the bottom! I even put this on top of it!" I said, holding up a glass paperweight. I started racing around the room, even though I knew I hadn't put the file anywhere else, searching desperately, pulling books out, throwing cushions and papers around, hurling drawers open, going through their contents.

It was true. We looked everywhere, but the Perdita folder was nowhere to be found.

"They were after that information!" I yelled. "My diary had been opened at the page where I mentioned the Perdita file! And I can't believe I helped them find it. I made it easy for them. I could kick myself!"

I grabbed the spy pen and yelled at it. "OK, you thieving criminals! You listen to me. We're on to you. We're coming after you and I'm going to get my Perdita file back, so you'd better watch out!"

"Very impressive, Winter," said Boges. "But my bet is that nobody is even monitoring that bug anymore. They already got what they wanted. Save your breath."

"Why were they after Perdita?" Cal asked. "And we still haven't found out who the Drowner is."

"And are they related?" Ryan asked. "Or just two different kinds of weird?"

"You mean you don't know?" asked Boges, as we all swung around to look at him. "The Drowner is besties with Perdita," he said, keeping a straight face. "We're chasing down the perfect mystery couple!"

Ryan punched his arm before I could. "OK, Mr. Clever. Where do you reckon we start?"

"I'm thinking, I'm thinking. Give my brilliant brain a chance to figure it out." He picked up the spy pen. "This is cheapskate stuff. You can buy it in electronic shops. They're not really used by professionals—but I guess they didn't want to risk putting in something better. Winter could have walked in on them while they were installing something more sophisticated."

"They think they're just dealing with a bunch of kids," said Ryan, "so they're just using kiddie stuff?"

"I hate the thought that some thief was sneaking around my study," I said, shivering. "It gives me the creeps."

"Well, the good news is their observation post would have to be very close by," Boges said. "This signal wouldn't carry very far."

"Continue please, Sherlock," I commanded, rallying from my shock and anger. "Where exactly are you heading with all this?"

"I'm heading . . . somewhere very local. They would just need a car . . . or a nearby shed."

"So," I said slowly, "we should search around my place?"

Boges turned to me. "Noticed anything unusual in your street lately? Any cars that seem out of place?"

"Now that you mention it," I said slowly, "there has been a strange-looking van parked across the street for a few days. I remember it because it had an Irish sticker, *Beautiful Kilkenny*, on the back window."

"Let's check it out," Boges said.

I grabbed my flashlight.

Two minutes later, the four of us were standing around an abandoned old van parked on the high point of the hill in Mansfield Way. There was a parking ticket stuck to the windshield. I did a quick check up and down the street, then deftly dealt with the lock on the driver's side.

Swiftly, I unlocked all the other doors. "Ballet and art weren't the only things I learned living with Sligo," I muttered.

I switched on the flashlight and ran the beam across the front seats of the van as Boges slid in for a closer look.

"Look at these newspapers—they're just from the last couple of days," he said, moving across into the driver's seat. "Someone's been sitting here reading and doing a lot of crosswords."

Ryan and Cal flung open the rear doors and crawled into the back of the van. "OK," Ryan said. "Let's turn it inside out, see if they left a calling card."

"There's nothing much in the back, I'm afraid," Cal called out as they rummaged around. "Any luck up front?"

There was a plastic bag hanging off the gear-shift as a makeshift trash bag. Carefully, I tipped out the contents onto the passenger seat. Three empty plastic sandwich wrappers had "packed on" dates that suggested the spy had been monitoring my place for at least three days. This did not make me feel any better. There was, however, no empty wrapper with today's date.

"You were right, Boges," Ryan said. "He didn't need to listen anymore because he'd found the file." Normally, Boges would've grinned and said something like, *I'm pretty much always right*, but today, what with everything that had happened, he let the joke go.

"Hey, look at this!" I yelled, plucking some-thing from the corner of the floor mat near the accelerator. I held it up. A Triple Mint chewing gum wrapper, balled up in exactly the same way as the wrapper in my study.

"Snap!" said Ryan. "This has got to be our guy. Is there anything else in that plastic bag?"

"Only some ripped paper." Boges spread the pieces out. We could see that there was writing, but it had been torn over and over.

"Let's go back to your place," Cal said, "and see if we can fit these pieces of paper together. Look at what we've got."

"OK. I want to find out how this person got into my house," I said angrily. "And make sure they can't ever do it again."

We checked every door and window of my place. It didn't take us long to find the weak spot. One of the laundry room windows was just a little open at the top and there were dirty fingerprints along the top of the dusty frame. "He's been coming in and out through here," I said, "and I thought that window was locked. It definitely is now." I closed it firmly and locked it. "I'll lock the laundry room door too, just in case."

We sat around the glass-topped coffee table in my living room. "Let's try to put this paper together," I said. "It looks like something from a business notepad." Eventually, we fitted the pieces back together like a jigsaw and got tape to hold it all together. Someone had scribbled:

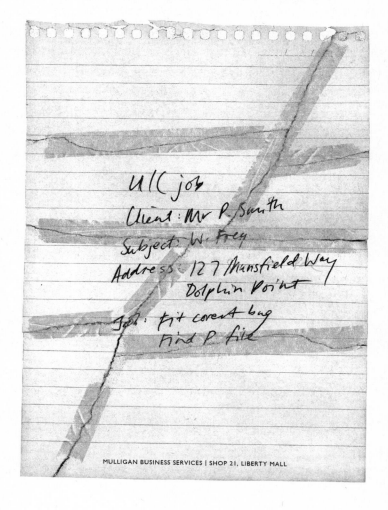

"It's the job description, the job he was doing," I cried. "Spying on me!"

But the best thing of all was the small print running along the bottom of the notepaper: *Mulligan Business Services, Shop 21, Liberty Mall.*

"I'm pretty sure U/C means 'undercover'," Boges said. "Tomorrow we'll practice a little surveillance of our own, on Mulligan Business Services. Maybe we'll get lucky and find a few answers."

"But why is this P. Smith paying money to spy on me and get hold of the Perdita file? Who is he? Is he the Drowner?" No one could answer my questions.

"Are you going to stay here tonight, Winter?" Cal asked, his face still creased with concern.

"Yep, now that we know my spy has gone, I'd rather be home . . . but thank you," I said, squeezing his hand.

DAY 3

28 days to go . . .

Home
Mansfield Way, Dolphin Point

8:02 am

I was going to meet the boys at Liberty Mall. Cal and Boges had a free period on Monday mornings, and Ryan's class was at the local library working on group assignments—he didn't think he'd be missed. Being homeschooled had its advantages. As long as I got my assignments done for my tutor, I could organize my time pretty freely.

I grabbed a coffee and an apple, my mind going crazy trying to figure out what the warning about the Drowner and the theft of the Perdita folder could mean. I got nowhere. I needed more information—much more.

I paused in the hallway near the big stained-glass front door where a small half-circle table held a photo of me and my parents, taken about a week before their deaths. They look so happy—and so do I, smiling up at my dad. On the way out of the house, I touched the picture softly, whispering, "Hi there, Mum and Dad. Look after me?" They smiled back at me.

I grabbed my jacket and a beret and automatically checked for my locket around my neck. I was ready for anything.

Mulligan Business Services
Liberty Mall

8:43 am

The four of us hurried towards the escalator that took us up to the first level of the mall. The information map displayed Shop 21, Mulligan Business Services. "Look!" I said to the others as we stepped off the escalator. "That coffee shop is Shop 18. We're close!"

Mulligan Business Services turned out to be a small storefront, sandwiched between a lawyer's office and a florist.

"What do we do now?" asked Ryan.

"We wait and we watch," Cal said.

"What about some hot chocolate while we do that?" asked Boges. "You know how boring surveillance can be."

The small cafe was noisy with people having

breakfast and coffee. We sat at a table with a view of the door of Mulligan's through the leaves of the shiny indoor plants that shielded cafe customers from passersby. A couple at the next table made loud remarks about people who should be at school, so Boges started giving a totally incomprehensible lecture on quantum mechanics and we all nodded along wisely, as if we knew what he was talking about.

9:52 am

As we kept watch through the leaves, we finally saw a stout man, wearing rimless glasses, an open-necked shirt and sports jacket, walk up to the front door of Mulligan's. He unlocked the door, pushed it open and walked in, leaving the keys dangling in the lock.

"For someone who breaks into other people's houses, his own security is garbage," muttered Ryan from across the table.

"Hey, look!" said Cal. "He's come back out and closed the door, with the keys still in it. Don't look now . . . he's coming in here!" As the man stood at the counter, waiting behind a few other people to give his order, I kicked Cal under the table.

"Now's our chance! Quick! We've got a few minutes while he waits for his coffee. Ryan, you stay here and watch. Don't let him go back into his office until we're out of there. Delay him if you have to. Cal, Boges, let's go!"

Leaving Ryan at the table, we hurried out of the cafe and dashed over to the closed door with the keys hanging in it. No one was paying any attention to us, everyone too busy hurrying to work. The key turned easily and we darted inside.

It was a small one-room office, with a desk, a couple of chairs and some filing cabinets.

"We've gotta find that file, guys," I said, turning my attention to the filing cabinets. I tugged on the drawers, but they were locked.

The desk had a heap of folders on it, none of them mine, and what looked like a two-way radio system. Cal was searching the shelves above the desk, and Boges was working his way through the drawers on the right-hand side of the desk while I turned my attention to the drawers on the left.

Cal's phone buzzed. "It's Ryan," he hissed. "The guy's digging in his pockets to pay. We've gotta get out of here!"

I doubled my speed. The first thing I found was a handwritten check for $1,500 with an illegible signature. Although unreadable, something about the writing seemed familiar and I wondered where I'd seen it before.

"We have to leave now!" said Cal. "There's no other way out of this place. And he probably knows your face, Winter."

I pulled open the last drawer. There it was, my Perdita folder! I snatched it, bashing the drawers closed. Boges had done the same as Cal straightened the files on the shelves and the three of us hurtled towards the door. We cracked it open and peeked out. There Mulligan was, only a few yards away, outside the cafe, talking to Ryan. Any moment he might turn around and see us coming out of his office.

"Come on!" I hissed, pushing the boys out the door. I pulled it closed until I heard the lock click. Seconds later, the three of us strolled innocently past the detective who was still talking with Ryan, and around the corner.

I caught snatches of conversation: " . . . best to finish school . . . private investigator's license . . . quite a lot of law . . . "

A few minutes later, Ryan caught up with us. "That was close," he grinned. "I had to practically block his way and pretend that I was desperately interested in becoming a private investigator. His name is Arnold Mulligan. Did you get the file?"

"You bet," I said. "Let's get out of here!"

I couldn't wait to get home and have a look

at the Perdita file, but the others had to go to school. They made me promise I'd wait until they were free later in the day.

To keep myself from peeking, I went to the library to research an assignment that Miss Sparks had been hassling me to hand in.

Home
Mansfield Way, Dolphin Point

4:14 pm

I heard Cal's motorbike outside and I put the folder down on the dining table where everyone could see it. A few minutes later, Boges and Ryan turned up too. With everyone crowded around, I slowly opened the folder and looked at the first page, my heart beating with excitement and apprehension. There *had* to be something interesting in this file for someone to have paid to get their hands on it.

"Looks very legal, whatever it is," said Cal, looking over my shoulder. "Looks like title deeds or something."

At first, it didn't make any sense and I felt disappointed. It was just some boring old legal document. What had I been expecting? But as I read further, it started to become clear.

TRANSFER 9542

Certificate of Title

LANDS ACT 1900

This title is to certify that <u>Charles G Frey</u> is now the sole proprietor of the property and land located at 428 Clifftop Drive, Deception Bay, hereby known as the 'Perdita' estate.

Dated this Fifteenth day of March 1997

REGISTRAR

I looked at the others. "Perdita isn't a *person*," I said, "it's a *property*—a house!"

"Must be some kind of mansion—worth squillions—for someone to go to so much trouble to steal the deeds!" Ryan said. "Maybe they were hoping that you would never know about it, with the masses of paperwork you had to go through. I'll bet it's a palace with amazing bathrooms and swimming pools and tennis courts and a helicopter pad on the roof."

"And a Lear jet parked in the huge driveway!" Boges added, catching Ryan's enthusiasm. "You can take us for a ride, dude," he said, turning to Cal.

"I'm going to Google it," I yelled, running upstairs. It didn't take me long. "Hey! I've found the house. Come and have a look!"

The others leaned closer to the picture on the screen of my computer. I zoomed in on the property, but I could only see a tiny bit of the roof because it seemed to be surrounded by lots of trees. Perdita stood by itself at the end of a long headland, quite close to the edge of an escarpment. When I zoomed back out, I could see waves at the bottom of the cliff and the beach running along the coast.

"That must be Deception Bay," I said. "Wonder why it's called that?"

"Looks like a really fantastic spot," Boges said. "Pity we can't see the house clearly."

"It's heaps overgrown, but it could be awesome!" said Ryan.

I turned to the boys and gave them a wide smile. "So who feels like a road trip?"

DAY 7
24 days to go . . .

Cal's House
Flood Street, Richmond

5:53 pm

The week crawled by and I hardly saw the others. I tried to take my mind off everything by working on my assignment and looking forward to dinner with Cal's family before he left for flight school.

Finally Friday night came, and I arrived just as Boges and Ryan turned up. Ryan had brought flowers for Mrs. Ormond and we enjoyed her meal of spaghetti Bolognese, followed by a chocolate mud cake I'd made for the occasion.

"Will you be a real pilot when you get back, Cal?" Gabbi asked.

"I wish," Cal said, mussing up her hair. "I'll just be more experienced and ready for more training later." Mrs. Ormond smiled at us all. It looked like she was finally able to let Cal out of her sight without worrying that something terrible was going to happen.

I sighed, hoping that we wouldn't be worrying her with anything else.

"He'll be back soon, Winter," Mrs. Ormond said, misreading my apprehension. I smiled and nodded. It was better she didn't know about the Drowner, whoever he was.

10.22 pm

I was putting the leftover cake in the fridge when I overheard Cal talking to Boges just outside the kitchen.

"I hate to leave, but I know you'll see it through, whatever it is."

"Dude, you can rely on me a thousand percent."

As they walked in and saw me, Cal came over and gave me a hug.

"I can look after myself, you know," I reminded him.

"I know . . . but a little Boges backup goes a long way," he smiled.

We walked outside, where Ryan was waiting to take me home.

We paused in the driveway. "Repro called me—finally," Cal said. "I've given him everyone's numbers so you might be hearing from him. OK?"

"I hope we see him down there."

"You made a promise that you'll call if things get dangerous. Don't forget. And let me know the second anything surfaces about this Drowner guy."

"I will," I said. "I'd better go, but don't worry about me—you just concentrate on your flying lessons and I'll see you soon."

"Thanks, Winter. I'll be back in no time." He gave me one last hug and I could see that his eyes were troubled.

Cal watched me get into Ryan's car and waved us off down the street.

DAY 8

23 days to go . . .

Home
Mansfield Way, Dolphin Point

10:49 am

I packed the Perdita file right at the bottom of my scram bag. I'd gotten the idea from Sligo, who always had a hidden bag full of money, clothes and a passport, ready to scram overseas if the law—or his enemies—got too close. Now my overnight bag was always ready with spare toiletries, a towel and soap, some clothes, matches and a powerful flashlight. I threw in some mosquito repellent and last of all, I hid a bundle of cash in a hole in the lining.

The three of us fit into Boges's truck with me in the middle. Our gear for the weekend was piled up in the back. Ryan had thrown in his climbing gear too, just in case those nearby cliffs offered some good climbing opportunities.

I was feeling much better about everything

now that we were on the road. I had two good friends with me and a new property to inspect, so I didn't mind too much that Cal wasn't with us. But I struggled to keep from wondering why someone wanted this place so much they were desperate to get their hands on the deeds . . . and the mystery of the Drowner.

Abercrombie Village

12.32 am

In an hour and a half we had arrived in the neighborhood. Boges slowed down so we could look at the occasional luxury house that sat perched along the high right-hand side of the road. Mostly there was just bushland, dotted here and there with a shack, or a modest beach house. On our left, the huge expanse of the ocean stretched away as far as we could see.

We stopped and had some fresh fish and chips for lunch at a little place on the short main street of Abercrombie—the closest village to Deception Bay. I noticed a small grocery store next door, so we ducked in to buy supplies. I added detergent and cleaning stuff to the growing pile of food, thinking they might come in handy at some point—who knew what kind of state the house might be in.

While the woman behind the counter put everything into bags, I looked around the tiny, densely packed shop. It was more like a general store, with fishing tackle, work boots, hats and toiletries for sale. On a wall was a barometer and a very fancy thermometer, and I could see where the owner had been keeping statistics on rainfall and the weather on an official-looking chart. I guessed that many small shops in somewhat remote locations operated as weather stations for the Department of Meteorology, sending in local reports every day.

The woman, who looked tired and strained, seemed to be keeping a close watch on me all the time and, noting my interest, she nodded in the direction of the weather charts.

"We need to watch the weather around here, and not just to report it . . . the storms can be diabolical." She began adding up the bill. "So what brings you three young people to our little town?"

"I'm looking at houses," I said, not wanting to give too much away.

"You look a bit young to be buying a house," said the woman, frowning. "Nothing around here for sale—well, nothing you'd want to buy, at least."

I sensed that the woman was fishing for information. "We'd better be going," I said, smiling at her and picking up the rest of our order.

The woman gave me a very direct look. "Be careful," she said, then seemed to get flustered, turning away and pretending to dust the already spotless counter with a cloth. "I mean," the woman was saying, "be careful how you drive. There's a lot of unpaved road further on."

"Uh, thanks for the tip . . . bye now."

"By the way, my name's Rose."

"Pretty name," I said as we gathered up our bags and hurried back to the truck.

"What was all *that* about?" asked Boges.

"I don't know," I said. "It was like she was trying to find out why we were here. But she looked worried as well."

"Why didn't you tell her your name?" Ryan asked.

I shrugged. "Not sure. Just a bit wary, I guess."

1:51 pm

We continued on our drive up the steep winding hills until we met Clifftop Drive itself, turning along the road with breathtaking views out across the water. After a while, the houses thinned out until we hit unpaved dirt track, just as the shopkeeper, Rose, had said. The scenery changed to untouched bushland.

"Perdita must be a long way from anywhere," said Boges.

Almost as he spoke, a car shot out of an obscured driveway on our right, heading straight for us! It was about to plow straight into the driver's door—and Boges!

As I yelled out and grabbed the dashboard, Boges slammed his foot down and Ryan yelled as the truck surged ahead. I felt a thud at the back as the other car clipped our tailgate and ran into a tree on the opposite side of the road.

"What an idiot!" Boges yelled. "Came out of nowhere!" He jumped out to inspect the damage. I recovered from my shock quickly and scrambled out after Ryan, concerned about the driver in the stalled car across the road. I didn't have to worry for long. The driver's door was flung open and a girl in jeans and a khaki shirt, who looked only a bit older than me, flounced across the road and stood with her hands on her hips.

"What do you think you're doing?" she yelled at Boges, her cheeks red with anger and her thick tawny hair whipping around her in the wind.

"I could ask the same of you!" shouted Boges, pointing to the driveway she'd just exploded from. "You're supposed to yield when you enter a road from a driveway, not just barge out as if you're the only person in the world!"

"But no one comes out here apart from me!" she argued.

The girl, who would have been quite pretty except for the anger that screwed up her face, swung around, heading back to her battered old blue station wagon. It was jammed up against a large tree, but she still jumped into it and tried to start the engine. We heard the motor turning uselessly, over and over.

"She's going to flood it if she doesn't stop," said Ryan.

"Serves her right!" said Boges. "I'm going to go and give her a piece of my mind!"

Now that the shock had worn off, I was feeling pretty angry too. Ryan and I charged over behind Boges as he approached the stalled car.

The girl was hunched over the steering wheel and I suddenly wondered if she was crying. Boges's angry demeanor fell away as he looked with concern into the driver's window.

"Are you OK?" Boges asked.

"I don't know how I'm going to manage," the girl said, lifting her head from the steering wheel. "I can't afford to get it fixed. I can't afford to get it towed. Now I can't even get away from here!"

It was then that I noticed how threadbare and patched her jeans were and her khaki shirt was badly frayed at the collar. Her face was wet with tears and her blue eyes were filled with anxiety. "This car is about the only thing I've got now—the only thing I had."

She straightened her shoulders and blew her nose on a tissue. "And now it's wrecked! I don't know what I'm going to do."

I moved closer to the driver's window. "I'm Winter," I said, thinking of Ryan's climbing ropes in the back of the truck. "We could give you a tow. At least back up your driveway."

I looked at the sagging gates of the driveway she'd just raced out of. They seemed to be permanently propped open, supported by two stone pillars with the words "Abercrombie House" carved on them. "You might be able to fix it."

"OK," she said without enthusiasm.

Half an hour later, we'd managed to tow the girl's car up the winding track to her house. Abercrombie House might once have been a fine old stone mansion, with elegant shutters on the French doors, but it now looked as if it had been partly demolished and most of the shutters lay on the ground. Stones from the upper story lay in scattered piles. I could see the sky through some of the roofing. Once we'd detached the ropes and packed them away, we turned around to find that the girl had vanished.

"What happened to her? She was right here," said Ryan. "Man, she dents your truck, Boges, we give her a tow and then she just disappears?"

"She could've at least said thank you," grumbled Boges. "Hmph."

2:43 pm

"It can't be much further," I said, trying to keep my eyes on the map I'd printed out as Boges negotiated deep potholes. "According to this, we're going to run out of road pretty soon because Perdita and Abercrombie House are the only properties on this end of the headland. After that, there's just the ocean."

Almost as soon as I'd spoken, Boges slowed down and pulled up next to a tumbledown fence covered in bushes. Beyond the half-collapsed fence, starkly bare European trees mingled with the canopies of huge old fig trees to create a wall of green jungle.

"There hasn't been another house since we left crash girl's place," I said, looking up from the map. "This must be it."

"Not too sure about Perdita being a luxury palace, then," said Ryan. "How do we get in?"

"Looks like there's a gate over there," I said, pointing to some stonework just visible through the heavy vegetation.

Boges drove closer until we could see the tops of two pillars, capped by a huge stone that joined them. "It looks like something from Stonehenge," said Boges.

"And possibly just as old too," I joked.

We climbed out to get a better look. The two pillars were actually part of a wall that rose beyond the fence—a forbidding facade of gray, lichen-covered stones. On the heavy, overgrown lintel stone I made out some carved letters: P E R D I . . . but the rest was obscured by a heavy vine that had woven itself in and around the stones.

"Perdita," I whispered under my breath. "We've arrived."

Perdita

3:04 pm

Slowly, the three of us walked towards the house. It was possible to imagine that once, a long time ago, a wide, impressive driveway had welcomed visitors to the property. Now weeds and the small suckers of eucalyptus trees grew through the cracks in the paving stones. On the left, there were the remains of paddocks, now dotted with small trees and shrubs, while on the right were dense, almost black-green cypress and other trees crowded together in a thick grove.

The house was of a strange design—basically

two stories, but with very unusual third stories added only at each end.

"I get it—it's the shape of an old-fashioned galleon," said Boges, "with those higher floors on each end. Although I've never seen a house shaped like this before."

It was true. With a few tall masts sticking up in the middle section and some sails and banners, Perdita would have looked like a Spanish galleon.

"It doesn't look to be as rundown as Abercrombie House, at least," said Boges.

"Well, the top levels look OK—" I said, when I was interrupted by shouting behind us.

"Hey! You kids! What do you think you're doing here?" Stomping up the ruined driveway was a weather-beaten man with a short gray beard and moustache, and stringy hair matted with salt. He was dressed in faded jeans, a worn-out shirt and had very tanned bare feet. The old man came up to us, hands on his hips, head cocked to one side, his shrewd eyes glittering.

"I'm inspecting my property," I said, "and these are my friends. What are you doing here?"

That seemed to take him aback, but only for a second. "You're not thinking of moving in?" he asked. "What would you want with a dump like this? A nice young lady like you?"

If there's one thing I can't stand, it's being

called a nice young lady, but before I could say anything, he went on. "The name's Jack Curlewis," he said, ignoring the black look on my face, "but everybody hereabouts calls me Curly. I kind of keep an eye on this place. Not that I need to, no one ever comes here. I do a bit of fishing, bit of prospecting, some odd jobs." He frowned. "But you can't be thinking of keeping a ruin like this! If it really is yours, I know someone who'll give you a very good price for it. Mind you, it looked very grand last century when Captain Green-lowe built it. Nowadays," he continued, with an unpleasant chuckle, "it's more like a ghost ship."

"I'm Winter Frey," I said and I didn't put out my hand for him to shake. "What's the problem with the house? Has it been vandalized?"

"Winter Frey, eh? Well, the house is neglected because nobody's lived here for ages. The garden's overgrown too, as you can see. But no, you don't need to worry about vandalism here. No one would *dare* to go inside there," he added in a whisper, pointing to the house. From an upper story, a tattered curtain blew through a broken windowpane.

"Too scared of you, eh, Curly?" asked Ryan, grinning.

Curly's eyes shifted from Ryan back to me. "Scared of a harmless old coot like me? What a joke! People don't come to this place because it's *haunted*. Bad things happened here a long time ago."

"What bad things?" I asked.

"Dreadful things. So bad that now—" he lowered his voice to a whisper "—she *walks*. Captain Greenlowe's daughter, Perdita. That's where the house gets its name, you know. Something terrible happened and she died. Locals around here call her the White Lady."

"You're not seriously telling me that you believe in ghosts?" I asked. "I hope I don't look like the sort of person who's scared off by silly stories."

"Yeah, are you kidding us?" asked Boges.

Curly gave us a sly look. "You suit yourselves. Don't say I didn't warn you." With that, he turned around and walked off, out the overgrown gate.

"That's the third weirdo local we've met," said Ryan. "Are they *all* loopy around here?"

"Maybe it's something in the water," Boges joked. "Come on, let's go meet the White Lady."

I let the boys walk ahead as I wondered about Perdita, Captain Greenlowe's tragic daughter. What had happened to her?

Worn stone steps led up to a black-and-white marble verandah that ran around the front and sides of the house as far as we could see. We stepped up onto it and I tested the wide front door, set between two panels of stained glass. It was locked, but the tall window on the right of the door was slightly open and with Boges and Ryan's help, I was able to open it wide enough to climb through. I straightened up, brushed the dust from my hands and looked around. In the fading daylight, the tall windows and the grand carved fireplace set deeply in the wood-paneled wall of the large front room were spellbindingly beautiful, despite the coating of thick dust. Like the stage setting for some wonderful play.

"Oh," I breathed, "it's magical!"

"*Was* magical," corrected Boges, as I let the boys in the front door.

Old-fashioned wallpaper festooned the walls, some of it peeling a little, and the floorboards creaked as we walked. Dust sheets shrouded lumps that looked like armchairs and other bits of furniture.

"Looks a bit spooky," said Ryan.

"I hate to break the spell," said Boges, "but how come that window you got through was unlocked?"

I took a closer look at the window and stepped back, alarmed. "It wasn't unlocked. It's been forced open. Look. You can see where the wood's splintered here. And those look like footprints in the dust," I said, pointing to a series of faint tracks across the room. "Someone's been in here quite recently."

"She walks!" Ryan reminded us. "But I didn't know ghosts left tracks . . . "

"Curly?" Boges asked.

"Could be. So why is he snooping around?"

"Curious, maybe," suggested Boges.

After checking out the main room, we went down the hallway. The footprints petered out so that it was impossible to tell where the intruder had snooped. Maybe it *had* simply been a nosy passerby.

We ventured into what remained of the kitchen, where a huge old-fashioned wood-burning stove stood at one end, and some battered pots and pans hung from hooks along the wall above it. The whole kitchen, like the rest of the house, was covered in layers of dust.

"This place needs a serious cleaning," I said. Past the pantry was the laundry room. Off the laundry room was an ancient toilet. I pulled the rusty chain and to my surprise, dirty water spluttered out in a noisy flush. "Hey, guys," I called to the others, "all mod cons here!"

We walked back through to the main staircase. "Let's explore upstairs," I said.

"Careful," said Boges. "*She* might be walking upstairs."

"I'll take my chances," I said, smiling. "Anyway, if she is, she should be paying me rent."
At the top of the stairs, there were several rooms that ran off the landing. Pushing open doors, we found dusty old bedrooms. Right at the end of the second floor, narrow wooden stairs led up to a square room with wide windows, bare of furniture apart from a round rug and a heavy chest which we couldn't open.

"That's mysterious," Ryan said.

"Wow, you can see all the way to the town from here," Boges said, his nose against the glass.

I went down the few steps back onto the main landing and walked up to the other end where another short set of stairs led to a similar room overlooking the sea. I stared out at the misty horizon, wondering if Perdita used to stand here waiting for Captain Greenlowe to sail back home.

The door nearest the top of the staircase hung crookedly from its hinges and I gave it a shove and walked in. This looked like the master bedroom, with a wide balcony outside the French doors. They were locked, but the big old key still stood in the lock and after a few twists and turns, it unlocked with a groan and I stepped outside. The balcony overlooked the oval driveway and the front of the house. From this vantage point, I could see a thick grove that seemed impenetrable, yet there seemed to be some sort of building deep in the center.

"Great view," said Boges, joining me on the balcony. He leaned forward, frowning. "What's that in the grove?"

"I was just wondering that. It was probably a nice park when it was first planted. Maybe it's a summer house in the middle."

We wandered back outside to take a better look at the grounds, walking past the grove to where the property ended at the edge of a steep cliff.

"You wouldn't want to be stumbling around here in the dark," said Boges.

I went further ahead and peered over. "Take a look at this!" Beneath us, about fifty yards down, a wide beach swept in a graceful curve to the north. "And look," I said as the others came up to join me, "there's Curly. What's he doing down there?"

Curly seemed to be finding something very interesting in the rocks right under the cliff face beneath us.

"Could be looking for bait," suggested Ryan.

I wanted to go down to the beach, but there wasn't enough light, so we got to work setting up a makeshift dining table and chairs from crates and old bits of wood that were lying around.

"So, why would anybody want this place so

badly?" Boges asked, as we spread our goodies in front of the roaring fire we'd built. "It'd cost a fortune to restore—even if you pulled it down and rebuilt it."

"I guess it'd take hundreds of thousands of dollars to get it into shape again," I said wistfully.

I'd brought the old newspaper clipping about the Drowner with me, and we talked about it and what the thirty days might mean, but didn't get anywhere. We were on a countdown, but to what? At least I felt safer being away from the city, and from where any more dodgy detectives, or worse, criminals called the Drowner, might easily find me.

9:27 pm

"Who wants hot chocolate?" Ryan asked, stretching as he stood up.

"Count me in," Boges said.

"Me too!" I sat there curled up in the old armchair, feeling completely at home in Perdita's big room with the fireplace crackling and the company of my friends. Just one thing was missing.

"It would be really good if Cal was here," I said.

"Only a few weeks," Boges reminded me, "and he'll be back." I sighed.

A horrible groaning from the hall shocked me. I sat bolt upright in my chair.

"What was *that*?" I jumped as Boges's voice whispered in my ear.

"What was that awful noise? Where is Ryan?" I cried. "Is he hurt?" I was halfway out of the chair when I stopped dead in my tracks. A terrifying, shrouded form loomed at the doorway, ghostly arms grasping at the air ahead of it. I screamed and Boges's face drained. The two of us stood like frozen statues.

The shrouded form suddenly threw back the moldy sheet, and Ryan jumped out, laughing his head off.

I pounced on him. "You rat bag, Ryan! You scared the living daylights out of me!" Boges joined in and together we tackled Ryan down to the floor. "Apologize! Or you'll suffer," I threatened him, sitting on his legs while Boges pinned him down. "You'll be tickled to death!"

"Apologize . . . or you'll die laughing!" said Boges, tickling viciously.

"OK, OK," Ryan gasped, between bursts of laughter, "I apologize. But, man, it was so worth it! You should have seen your faces!" That set him off again.

"Total garbage," said Boges. "I knew it wasn't a real ghost."

Ryan roared with laughter and I joined in. "Boges," I reminded him, "your face was as white as Ryan's sheet!"

I got up and dragged the old sheet that Ryan used out from under him, releasing a cloud of dust that made all of us cough and sneeze. Finally we calmed down.

That night, I snuggled down into my sleeping bag in the large front bedroom, excited at spending my first night in my "new" old house. I could hear Boges snoring away in the next room, and was surprised Ryan hadn't thrown anything at him yet.

I fumbled for my phone as I started to feel sleepy—I had just enough of a phone signal to send a message to Cal.

▤ Perdita is awesome. Rundown but v cool. Staying to check it out. Wish you were here. You'll love this place. Have fun with the fly boys! W x

DAY 10

21 days to go . . .

Perdita

7:15 pm

We spent most of the next two days cleaning up Perdita. It was a huge job, but with the three of us working at it and having fun, joking and teasing each other at the same time, the hours flew by each day.

We explored the long beach, having found a path down between Perdita and Abercrombie House. We brought back shells and driftwood for kindling and by Monday evening the old place was looking pretty good—at least downstairs.

"Don't get too comfortable," said Boges, clearing away some of the mess after dinner. "I want to leave in about half an hour. I've got a couple of big days coming up. I gotta cram in some assignments and help out my uncle, too. But then I'd like to come back again. What about you Ryan, Winter?"

"I didn't get to do any climbing and I want to try that cliff at the edge of the property," said Ryan. "It'd be good to get a chance."

"We should call Cal before we go," I said. And I did so, passing my phone around so that everybody had a chance to talk to him.

"It's great," Cal said, "but man, they work us hard. I miss having your help, Boges, with the navigation stuff."

"The great brain is at your disposal, dude. I'm only a phone call away."

Comfy in my favorite armchair once more, I realized I didn't want to go back to the city—I wanted to stay here, do more exploring, maybe find out more about my neighbor—aka "crash girl."

"This is the life," I said after a few moments. "I'm getting used to this place. Actually," I said, "I'd quite like to stay here a bit longer."

Boges frowned, looking up from packing his laptop. "It's a bit isolated, Winter. Are you sure? You won't have wheels till I get back."

"I'll be fine. I've lived alone a lot. And there's plenty to do here."

Boges wasn't convinced, but I packed them off back to the city, watching the red taillights disappear through the overgrown gate and up the road. All around me now seemed peaceful and still, but as I went to walk inside, a chill wind blew through the tangled overgrowth of the grove, like the sound of somebody sighing.

I closed the front door firmly behind me and locked it, glad that Boges had fixed the broken window frame. Just to be on the safe side, I dragged one of the huge old armchairs out of the front room and wedged it hard up against the front door.

After reading for a while, I bedded down for the night.

DAY 11

20 days to go . . .

Perdita

7:04 am

I was up early, excited by the prospect of having Perdita all to myself. It was a perfect day and I spent it very happily wandering the beach and exploring the local countryside.

Back at the house, I went through each room, checking out the remaining furniture and all the nooks and crannies. In the evening, Boges called to see how I was. "Fine," I told him, "just about to have dinner."

"Any sign of the White Lady?"

"No way," I laughed. The phone crackled. "I think we're losing reception. Guess I'd better go."

"Sleep tight, country girl."

"You too, city boy," I said, hanging up.

DAY 12

19 days to go . . .

Perdita

10:26 am

The following day, I walked all the way into the village because I'd run out of bread. I strolled through the small street, past a bank, the post office and a row of shops. The local people seemed friendly enough, but curious. When I ducked into the general store, Rose wasn't there, but I was lucky enough to score a lift back to Perdita with Rose's nephew Kyle, who was delivering mail. I got out at Abercrombie House and noticed the bank letter that Kyle shoved into the large metal mailbox.

I didn't do much for the rest of the evening— the long walk to the village had tired me out and I crashed early after dinner.

11:51 pm

Thud! I woke up with a start. What was *that*?

I jumped up, throwing the sleeping bag off me. Grabbing the flashlight, I crept to the door and opened it. There came a strange noise, like something scraping along the ground. I crept along the upper hallway, trying to pinpoint where the sound was coming from. At the top of the staircase I waited. The scraping came again. Downstairs! My heart was beating so hard I thought anyone in the house would hear it, but on silent bare feet, I made my way down the staircase and along the hall. Boges's warning came back to me as I suddenly realized I was completely cut off, miles away from anyone. Whoever this was, I was totally alone with them.

The sound seemed to be coming from the main room. I inched along the hallway and stood at the doorway, where Ryan had done his ghost number a few nights before. By the starlight from the windows, I could see the room was empty. And yet, the sound was coming from there. I crept in further.

Impossibly, the sound seemed to be coming from near the big old fireplace—from *inside the walls!*

I hated to admit it, but I was getting really scared now. But ghosts weren't real—everybody knew that. I cleared my head and thought hard. I'd heard of an insect called the deathwatch beetle that made these kinds of noises in walls. Could that be what it was? I tried desperately to think of a rational explanation.

Suddenly, the sound was above me on the second floor! I ran on tiptoes as fast as I could, back up the stairs, and waited, straining every fiber of my being to hear any sound. But all was silent. And then I heard a whistling sound and a thud from somewhere outside! What was going on around here?

I crept back to my bedroom and peered in. Of course it was empty and dark, with an even denser blackness beyond the windowpanes.

Hesitating, I stole over to the windows to look out. My jaw dropped! I blinked hard, not believing my eyes. My hand shaking, I opened the balcony doors and stepped outside.

What I saw made me doubt my sanity. It couldn't be . . . but it was.

11:58 pm

Inside the grove was the ghostly figure of a woman, hovering in the air. She was wearing a long white dress, her hair streaming over her shoulders, head turned to the side so that I couldn't see her face. Her transparent feet seemed to be about a foot from the ground. I stared in disbelief.

The apparition wavered before moving slowly forwards. As the ghost came closer, she turned her face towards me and I gasped in horror . . . it was a gaunt skull, with a hideous grin!

Crash!

I jumped in fright, then I realized I'd dropped the flashlight. I had to confront the apparition still glimmering in the blackness of the grove. I forced myself to hurry downstairs and outside.

I paused. The ghostly specter in white still shimmered through the trees. Ready to bolt at the slightest hint of danger, and fighting every instinct that said "Run!" I started to inch closer.

I don't believe in you, I kept chanting inside my head. *I don't believe in you!*

Through the branches, I caught a glimpse of the black pits of her eyes, which seemed to bore into me as I took each reluctant step in her direction and then, in a heartbeat—she vanished!

Only blackness loomed ahead of me. What had just happened? What had I seen? I approached the grove very cautiously. There was some fog and something else—a bad smell I couldn't place. I had just witnessed the impossible . . . a real ghost. I knew I wasn't dreaming, but I was scared. I hadn't liked the look of her at all—that ghastly grimace and those black eye sockets. And what of the knocking sounds? Was that her as well? I turned and bolted back into the house, locking the door, leaning against it and getting my breath back. All was silent—the house was as still as stone.

Slowly, I went upstairs again, shining the flashlight ahead of me. Everything was just as I had left it. I grabbed the sleeping bag and headed back downstairs to the front room where the fireplace still glowed. I crawled back into the sleeping bag and huddled up in the big armchair. No way was I going to sleep for the rest of the night.

DAY 13

18 days to go . . .

Perdita

6:53 am

I was wrong about not sleeping. My eyes flew open as dawn was breaking and birds were chirping loudly. My muscles protested as I stretched out—I was stiff from sleeping in a weird position in the armchair. As I yawned, the events of the night before flooded into my mind. The impossible had happened—I'd seen a ghost. I scrambled for my phone.

Boges's sleepy voice answered. But he was wide awake in seconds when he heard what I had to say. "Winter, are you sure?"

"Boges, I came within a few yards of her. And then right before my eyes, she just vanished."

There was silence as Boges tried to process this incredible information. "Look, Winter, I promised I'd help my uncle out today with some cleaning work. But I'll come as soon as I can, later on. There has to be some rational explanation. Have you told Cal about it?"

"No—it was too late last night and I don't want to worry him about something that he can't do anything about right now. I'm going to have a really good search around the place," I continued, "especially at the edge of the grove where I saw her. There might be some kind of hiding place that she could have slipped into." That explanation didn't satisfy me at all, but I had to tell myself something.

"I'll tell Ryan," said Boges, "and we'll call when we're on our way. I'll bring my ghost-busting gear."

"We'll also need some tools to hack through the grove to get in there. And *please* make sure you're here by tonight," I said. "I don't think I can do another night alone here." I shivered at the thought.

7:10 am

As the daylight grew stronger, I started my search. I walked across the driveway and over to the grove. There were still traces of the weird smell I'd noticed the night before. I pulled out my phone and went online searching for "ghosts and bad smells." There were quite a few references to foul odors and evil spirits, but my phone dropped out before I could get much further.

I looked over to where the specter had appeared. It was overgrown with very dense bushes and tree branches that were tangled together. I worked my way through the dense foliage, ignoring the prickles that caught at my T-shirt and scraped my skin. I stopped in the approximate position of last night's phantom. But there was nothing to show that anyone had been here. There were no broken twigs or scrapes in the bark. The hard leafy floor of the forest was untouched apart from where I'd stepped.

I couldn't go any further without tools. I turned around and started making my way back out.

Then I heard something. Immediately I stopped moving, although a branch was sticking uncomfortably into my hip. Someone was creeping around the driveway. As stealthily as I could, I pressed my way forward until finally I'd broken free of the dense undergrowth and was almost at the edge of the grove. I looked through some leaves to see someone on the verandah, peering in at the window. The figure turned.

Crash girl from Abercrombie House!

"What do you want?" I called out angrily.

"Argh! You nearly gave me a heart attack! I thought you were a ghost!" she yelled.

After what had happened last night, the thought of *me* being a ghost struck me as hilarious. I couldn't help it. All the pent-up tension exploded out of me and I stood there in my ripped T-shirt, laughing like a hyena with the girl staring at me as if I was a lunatic.

My crazy laughter was infectious and soon she was laughing too, although a little uneasily. "What exactly are we laughing at?" she asked.

Brushing the tears of laughter from my eyes, I hurried over to her. "Not you," I said. "It's a long story, I'm afraid."

"You know this place is haunted," she said, putting out her right hand. "I'm Harriet Abercrombie, by the way. I'm really sorry about the other day. I wasn't sure if anyone was here. I'm on my way to the beach and thought I'd have a look around."

I wondered briefly if it had been *her* feet that had left those footprints in the dust. I wondered if this girl might know something regarding Perdita's history. "Why don't you come in for some breakfast?" I said. "And then maybe I could come down to the beach with you."

A few minutes later, we munched on toast together in the big room with the sun shining in.

"Why is it called Deception Bay?" I asked.

"Because this particular bay looks a lot like the harbor entrance, which is a couple of miles north. In the old days, sailing ships sometimes sailed in here by mistake and ended up on the rocks, shipwrecked." She took another bite of her toast. "There are sixteen shipwrecks off the coast along here." Harriet hesitated. "I really am sorry about the car accident. It was my fault. I wasn't concentrating and no one ever comes down this road but me. By the way, where are your friends?"

"In the city," I said. "They'll be coming back later today."

"Well, I'd just had some really bad news when I shot out of the driveway like that. The bank called. They won't lend me any more money so I'll have to sell my farm. And then I thought the car was wrecked too. But it was OK after I fixed the radiator."

"What about your family?"

Harriet shrugged. "There's no one else but me. My father left when I was little. Mum was ill for a long time and then . . . after she died, I tried to run the place by myself. But I'm broke, I owe the bank and I can't get a buyer. I've been trying for ages. But there's this water problem . . . "

"Tell me," I said, warming to Harriet. Of all

people, I knew what it was like to try making a life all by yourself.

"Abercrombie House used to be a wealthy estate. It was one of the best-known farms on the coast. But a long time ago, the river that used to supply water to the property dried up. Now I have to rely on just rainfall and that's been pretty patchy over the last few years. I can't afford to put in another dam, and the one I have is so small that even after good rain, I only have water for a few months. I can't afford to stay there—the property is finished as a farm." She stood up, flushed in the face. "I'd better go. I've got a lot to pack up. I'm moving out in a few weeks."

"What about going down to the beach?"

"I'm sorry, I'm just not in the mood now, but thanks for breakfast." She paused before adding, "And please pass on my apologies to that guy who was driving the truck."

"Boges," I said.

"Yeah—him."

8:35 am

After saying goodbye to Harriet, I went back into the house and while I was changing, my phone chimed.

"Gabbi!" I said. "Great to hear from you. How's everything?"

"I'm OK. But I miss Cal loads."

"Me too, Gabs."

"He called last night, says he's working really hard. It's so boring here, with just Mum and me. My bestie's gone away with her parents for vacation. I want to come see you."

"Here?" I said, alarmed. I didn't want Gabbi to be terrified by a ghost.

"Except Mum won't let me," Gabbi continued. "She said I should spend time with people my own age."

"It's not very comfortable here, Gabs," I said, relieved. "There's no TV and there's not even a bathtub or a real kitchen. We cook over the fireplace and wash in a big tub in the laundry room."

"Cool! Just like camping!"

"Not quite," I said.

"Mum's calling. I gotta go."

"I'll call you soon," I promised.

I headed off to the beach. It seemed a long way down this time and I had to concentrate on what I was doing. But my mind kept wandering as I tried to make sense of the apparition from the night before. I wondered too if I could trust Harriet. Underneath all that, my nagging anxiety about the Drowner still occupied my thoughts.

Finally, I was clambering over the rocks that

gave onto the pure white sand of the long cove. Ahead of me, the waves rolled and crashed on the sand, and a stiff wind blew my hair into my eyes as I strode along. The beach was deserted, or so I thought, until I heard footsteps splashing behind me and turned to see Curly running through the edge of the water towards me, waving.

I waited impatiently until he puffed up to me. "You seem to be surviving OK all by yourself," he said.

I frowned, puzzled and wary. Had this strange guy been watching me? "Yes, I'm fine," I said shortly. "Why do you ask?"

Curly shrugged. "No reason. It was a bit blowy last night. Thought you might have had some trouble with rattling windows and banging doors—funny noises—that sort of thing."

Funny noises? I thought. What does he know about last night? "Nothing out of the ordinary," I lied. I turned to make my way back up the cliff path, but Curly kept up with me.

"Have you thought any more about selling the property?"

"I haven't thought about it at all," I said curtly. "The next property is for sale—Abercrombie House. It's got the same cliff-top views. Your friend should buy that place."

"Ah, I'm afraid they have their heart set on Perdita."

"That's a real shame because you know what? So do I. Now, if you'll excuse me, I have lots of things to do today."

"Are you staying there again tonight?"

Now I was on full alert. "Why are you so interested?"

Curly grinned, revealing missing teeth. If he thought that was going to disarm me, he was very mistaken. "Just being neighborly," he said. "If you're staying there, I can go fishing and bring you a nice flathead in the morning."

I started quickly back up the cliff path. "I'm allergic to flathead," I called back.

6:46 pm

Twilight was falling when I heard Boges's truck turning into the driveway. I ran out to meet the boys. "Am I glad to see you two!" I yelled with relief.

They'd brought heaps of provisions so we had a feast while I told Ryan and Boges about what had happened the night before.

"So it just vanished?" Boges asked.

"That's right. I was creeping along, getting closer and suddenly—" I clicked my fingers "—she was gone. Just like that."

"Awesome!" said Ryan.

"It didn't seem very awesome in the middle of the night," I said.

"You mentioned a bad smell, and some fog?" Boges helped himself to more food.

"Yep," I said. "So I checked online. Supposedly, bad ghosts sometimes leave bad smells."

"So do a lot of other things," Boges said, deep in thought. "Not sure about the fog, though. I wonder if she'll walk again tonight?"

"If she does," said Ryan, "we'll be ready for her."

I also filled them in about Harriet and told them about seeing Curly on the beach. As I spoke, my phone chimed again.

▯ Hope everything good with you? Crazy busy here . . . prac and tech study 25 hrs a day! Send me some pics? Call soon. Cx

I texted back:

▯ Everything fine. Hanging out with B and R. Miss you . . . chat soon 4 sure. Wx

I'd made a promise that I wasn't keeping. I tried not to feel too guilty as I hit "send."

"It just sounds odd," said Boges, as we cleared up the plates. "Curly's mate who's so keen to buy the property—plus someone who was desperate enough to get hold of the Perdita file to hire an investigator. Are we talking about two interested parties or could it be the same person?"

"And why wouldn't they just have bought the place before?" Ryan asked. "Sligo had the deeds. A buyer could just have approached him. Am I the only one smelling a rat?"

"Winter smelled a ghost already," laughed Boges.

DAY 17

14 days to go . . .

Perdita

2:32 pm

We'd spent the next few days hanging out and exploring. Ryan had brought some boards with him, so we tried the local surf, which turned out to be pretty good. There were also some great bush walks nearby.

Boges teased me mercilessly about the White Lady. "Are you sure about this ghost? How come she hasn't come back?"

"Maybe she doesn't like guys," said Ryan, and we all laughed.

I threw myself into the hard work of cleaning Perdita, and at the end of all our efforts, the old house was starting to look good. "It's called shabby chic," I explained to the boys. "People go to a lot of expense to get this look," I said, pointing out the unevenly colored walls, the scrubbed floors, the tall sparkling windows.

I was keen to get into the large chest with the jammed lid and drawers in the top room. Ryan and Boges chiseled away some of the wood and applied a lot of force. Finally, we were able to pull the top drawer open.

"What's this?" I asked, pulling out and opening a large dusty box to find a pile of jigsaw pieces inside.

"What they did before television and DVDs," said Ryan. "Let's try putting it together and see what it is."

"It's huge . . . there must be hundreds of pieces," I said. "We haven't got a table big enough."

"We can do it on the floor downstairs," Boges said. "It'll give us something to do at night while we're waiting for your imaginary ghost."

I gave Boges a gentle punch, and we carried the big box downstairs and tipped out the contents in a massive pile.

"Wow!" laughed Ryan. "Where on earth do we start?"

I pulled out a few pieces that looked like they went together along the bottom edge. We fooled around with the puzzle and had exactly six pieces in place when I decided I'd had enough, and went upstairs to bed. The boys bunked down in their room next door.

DAY 18

13 days to go . . .

Perdita

1:06 am

I woke in alarm. Boges was shaking me. I had been dreaming of my mother holding me, hugging me, but then she just faded away.

"Listen," he hissed, squatting beside me, his hand hooding the flashlight. Ryan was standing at the door.

"What is it?" I asked, fully awake now.

"Listen. Those noises."

I strained to hear and sure enough, there were weird rustling and knocking sounds, as if the walls of Perdita were alive—and breathing!

"That's what I heard the night the ghost appeared," I whispered back.

"It's like it's coming from the walls," Ryan whispered. "And the ceiling, too."

"*Now* do you believe me? Kill the light," I said,

and we were plunged into darkness as we groped our way down the staircase. We crept to the main room window to look outside.

Nothing.

And then suddenly, unbelievably, a burst of light and—she was there! Drifting and floating where I'd seen her almost a week ago. We all jumped in shock.

"I don't believe it!" Boges muttered under his breath. I heard Ryan gasp.

The ethereal specter hovered and wavered against the backdrop of the grove, just as she had before, with her head turned away from us. From somewhere, an unearthly howl arose, making my skin prickle.

"*What was that?*" Boges whispered. He was gripping my arm and I was gripping Ryan.

The ghostly figure slowly turned its head towards us and we were menaced by the black pits where the eyes should have been and the haunting skull grin.

"Sheesh! That's horrible!" Ryan's voice was strangled with fear. Then she was gone!

The deep silence exaggerated the sound of my beating heart. We stood there, transfixed, until Ryan said, "Right, so who's game to go outside with the flashlight and have a look around?"

I took a deep breath. "I guess I am. What about you, Boges?"

"Let's do it," he said. Boges switched the flashlight back on, and keeping each other close, the three of us crept outside and into the cold air of the night. We kept going until we came right up to the spot where we had seen the apparition.

"There's that smell again," I said, sniffing the air.

"I'm having some serious doubts about this ghost," said Boges, as he sniffed around nearby.

"Man!" said Ryan. "It was just here. We all saw it!"

"We saw *something*," said Boges. "Let's go inside. It's really cold out here."

1:41 am

We huddled around the remnants of the fire.

"OK, Boges," I said, carefully watching his face in the firelight. "You're the scientist. What do you think is going on?"

"You said you were going to bring ghost-busting gear," said Ryan. "Did you?"

"You bet I did," Boges smiled.

"Where is it?" I asked.

"Right here," he said, tapping the side of his head. "In my prodigious brain box."

"Ah, your modesty," said Ryan, grinning. "Glad you haven't forgotten it."

"Let's figure out what we know," Boges said, ignoring the jibe. "Now, what would you say our ghost was made out of?"

"Some sort of ghosty stuff?" said Ryan. "Stuff you can walk right through."

"Yeah," I agreed. "Like mist or smoke."

"And you said it was a bit foggy when you went out to look for her the first time, Winter?" Boges added.

"So she's made out of fog?" Ryan asked. "Is that what you're suggesting?"

Boges didn't say anything for a while. "I'm not sure, I need to take a closer look before I start laying out my theories. I'm going back to bed for a few more hours' sleep," he finally yawned. "Somehow I don't think there'll be any more apparitions tonight. Let's sleep on it, and tomorrow we'll do a real search."

Despite our complaining, Boges refused to say any more without sleep. Annoyed, but relieved I now had witnesses, I had no choice but to wait until morning.

9:19 am

In the morning, we were eager to search the grove.

"OK," said Boges, handing out the hatchets

and clippers he'd brought with him. "We're going to stay pretty close together and we're going to search around the area where we saw the 'ghost' last night. We're going to do a fingertip search, just like the cops do. That means covering every single square inch of ground. Got it?"

It took us over an hour to make any headway, but as we cut and hacked our way, we checked out every bit of the overgrown ground.

Eventually I spotted something gleaming, and I pushed and shoved until I could get close enough to retrieve it. I called out to the others as I picked it up. It was a cylinder, like an empty cartridge shell, only larger and wider.

"What's that?" asked Ryan. "It looks like someone's been firing bazookas!"

"They've been firing something," said Boges.

"Is this some kind of pre-packed concentrated ghost mix?" I asked, pointing to the empty shell.

"Winter, this is the shell of a smoke flare. Depending on how much combustible material you put in it, it creates very dense smoke."

"I don't get it," said Ryan. "OK, so it smokes for a while, but how does the smoke make itself into a ghost?"

"It doesn't," said Boges. "It makes a screen that images can be projected onto."

"Like a movie?" I asked.

"Exactly like a movie. Do you remember the whistling sound you said you heard? That was the flare whizzing through the air, which also created the bad smell. Then all that's needed is a video projector pointed at the smoke and there's your ghost."

"Hang on a minute," I said. "Do you mean someone was in the house using a video projector?" I thought for a split second. "I bet I know where he was!" I turned and ran back into the house and up the stairs, hearing Boges and Ryan charging after me. I ran up to the third floor lookout room facing the garden. Sure enough, on the windowsill were fresh scrape marks in the dust.

"So," I said, "he had the video projector set up here, then he projected some ghost footage onto the smoke screen."

"Spot on!" said Boges, his face alight with enthusiasm. I grinned as I saw Ryan looking at me with admiration.

"That's why she went through the exact same routine the second time," I said. "He just repeated the footage."

"I wondered how come you were so brave about a ghost, Boges," Ryan teased.

"But what about that weird knocking and scratching in the walls? How do you explain that?" I asked.

Boges shook his head. "Sorry," he said, "I may be brilliant, but sometimes even a genius needs a little time to figure things out."

"We didn't find anything else," I reminded him, "no clues as to who might be trying to frighten me out of the place. We need to gather more intelligence first, and I've got an idea how. We should have a chat with my neighbor."

"Crash girl? No way!" said Ryan.

"Good idea," said Boges sarcastically.

"Her name's Harriet," I said defensively. "And she's lived here most of her life, so she's probably got a lot of local knowledge. How about a neighborly visit?"

Abercrombie House

11:26 am

We decided to walk to Abercrombie House. We went up the winding driveway to the old colonial stone mansion—what was left of it. The house stood on a slight rise with a few ancient rose bushes growing along the front. To the left was a wide, dry gully that ran the length of the house and beyond. Several chickens scattered at our approach. Across the gully, I could see the stooped figure of Harriet, working in a vegetable garden. As I called out and waved, she made her way over, her hair pulled back from her face under a knitted beanie—clearly dressed for work in a checked shirt and overalls.

I introduced her properly to Ryan and Boges and she shyly shook hands, excusing herself for the soil that clung to her fingers. "I've been digging potatoes," she explained. "Please come in. I'll make us something to drink."

We went down a dim hallway to a big kitchen at the back of the house.

"We brought these over," I said, placing some chocolate cookies and cheeses on the kitchen table. "Boges bought far too much for us," I lied. "I was hoping that you might be able to tell us a little bit about the local history."

"Oh yes?" Harriet said as she poured boiling water into a teapot.

"Harriet," I said, munching into a chocolate cookie, "some very strange things have been going on at Perdita lately."

"What sort of things?" Harriet asked, her brows contracting into a frown. "I did wonder when you acted pretty weird the other day, coming out of that grove looking like a ghost."

"Actually, I was *looking* for a ghost—well, evidence of how the ghost had happened."

"You saw the White Lady?"

"I think I'd better explain," I said. I told Harriet about the scary noises and the ghost, and how we'd finally figured out what had really happened.

"But why?" she asked, exactly echoing our own questions. "Why would someone be doing this to you?"

We told her about the Perdita file—about how it had been stolen and how we'd gotten it back. "You're so lucky to have such good friends," she said to me. "Do you know much about the history of Perdita?" she asked.

"Only that Captain Greenlowe built it over a hundred years ago for his daughter and she died in tragic circumstances."

"Well, there are two versions of the story," said Harriet. "One is that Perdita Greenlowe and Daniel Abercrombie, my great-grandfather, were hounded out of the country by Captain Greenlowe. They were in love, but he had forbidden their marriage after a terrible falling out with Daniel's father, Frederick Abercrombie, probably because of a dispute over the property boundaries. The second version is much darker."

"Uh-oh," I said, guessing. "The ghost story?"

"You got it! In that version, Captain Greenlowe, insane with rage about his daughter's relationship with Daniel Abercrombie, murdered Perdita and then said that she'd taken her own life. The story goes that she can't rest because of her tragic end. The Captain himself was said to have become obsessed with the house. He fussed over the grove in particular, ignoring his responsibilities, making enemies of the wrong kind of people, and ran the estate into the ground. And that's why the house is cursed and anyone who lives there is driven away."

"Someone else must know that version," said Boges, "to go to the trouble of making the ghost appear."

"And it gets even worse than that," said Harriet. "Captain Greenlowe cursed the whole Abercrombie family, swearing that the property would fall into wrack and ruin and that the farm would never prosper again. Not long afterwards, the stream that used to run past the house started drying up. My great-grandfather moved away, and ended up marrying my great-grandmother Blanche. By then, the Captain had passed away, but his curse remained. When my parents moved us back to the family estate, nothing had changed." Harriet gave a deep sigh.

"Wow, heavy stuff," Ryan said.

"Yeah, I'm really sorry to hear that, Harriet," Boges said gently. "But all that still doesn't explain why someone would want to terrorize

Winter," he added, "and try to scare her off so she sells Perdita."

"Well, there is one more thing I can think of," said Harriet. "There were rumors that Captain Greenlowe was a smuggler. But when the police raided the house, they could never find any evidence. He was also rumored to know the location of a ship that wrecked nearby." She looked up from her cup of tea. "A lot of the locals still talk about that shipwreck, the Windraker, full of gold coins that never reached their destination."

"A treasure ship wrecked near Deception Bay?" I asked.

Harriet nodded. "It's just local legend, nothing more." She stood up, signaling it was time for us to leave. "I'd love to chat more," she said, "but I've got a lot of packing to do."

As we walked outside, Harriet pointed to the dry gully running past the house. "That's the reason I have to go," she said. "It used to be a really reliable stream which watered this whole property. But now, it's all dried up. I've never seen it flowing, I've only ever seen it in a picture." She ran back inside and came out with an old, faded sepia photograph. A group of people dressed in old-fashioned clothes stood smiling by the house. Beyond them was the stream.

"Now look at it," she said, as we all turned to the dry riverbed. "I've given up hoping for a miracle," she said, "although there are other rumors . . . about those strange noises in the walls of the house—" Harriet suddenly stopped speaking.

I waited expectantly for her to finish. This was exactly the sort of information we needed.

"What sort of rumors?" I prompted. But something had changed; Harriet's face was closed.

"Oh, just silly talk. Now I really must go." She took the photograph out of Ryan's hands and flashed a quick smile. "Thanks for coming to visit." With that, she hurried inside.

Perdita

12:52 pm

As the three of us walked back, I was deep in thought. "Harriet was going to tell us something about the knocking in the walls, but she stopped herself."

"She knows more than she's saying," said Ryan.

"Maybe. She's a bit of an enigma," said Boges.

"I thought you only found those in zoos," joked Ryan.

"I think we need to get serious with our investigation," said Boges, ignoring Ryan's quip. "There's something going on and I want to know what it is."

As we walked back inside, I could see the determination on my friends' faces. It mirrored my own. "Let's go right back to the beginning," I said.

"You mean the Perdita file?" asked Ryan, his face showing the same resolute focus I'd often seen in Cal.

I nodded. I opened the file. We crowded around as I turned the pages. We saw the documentation transferring the property from my parents' possession to Sligo as trustee for me. The property transfers went back quite a way. Slowly, understanding dawned on me. "My parents didn't buy this place," I said, pointing to some older documents, "they *inherited* it. It was a family property on my father's side. Look, these rate notices go back over seventy years. That's in my grandparents' time."

Then I noticed something glued on the back inside cover of the file—an old envelope. I lifted the flap and pulled out a worn sheet of paper. "What's this?" I wondered. It was a peculiar drawing. I passed it to Boges and Ryan so that they could have a good look.

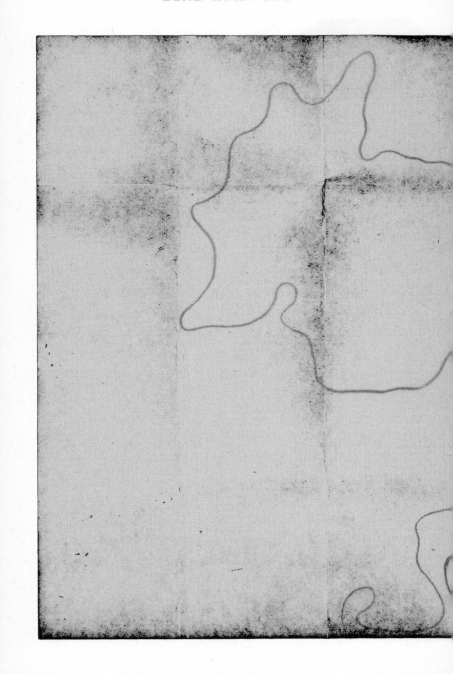

"It looks a bit like a ghost," said Boges.

"Ha! You've got ghosts on the brain!" I laughed. Looking closer, the shapes still seemed to make no sense. It looked as if someone had been interrupted halfway through drawing something.

"And that looks like an 'M' there," said Ryan, pointing. He was right. A faintly drawn M was marked next to two circles.

"Maybe it's just meaningless doodling," I said, folding the page and slipping it back in the envelope.

"But why would someone store it so carefully in the file if it was completely meaningless?" Ryan asked. It was a good question. "Everything to do with this place seems to involve a mystery."

"Whoever is after this place is after the secret it holds," I agreed.

"But we're going to beat them to it," Ryan said.

"I wonder," I said slowly, "if it really is about the Windraker and all that gold."

"We need to ask a few more questions," said Boges. "Time for a trip into town tomorrow."

DAY 19

12 days to go . . .

Abercrombie Village

2:49 pm

Rose looked up in surprise as we walked into the store. "Hi, Rose," I said. "My name is Winter and these are my friends, Ryan and Boges."

"You're the young people staying at Perdita!" she said. "I didn't expect—"

Then she lowered her voice, looking behind her where a curtain swung in a doorway. Was she about to say that she didn't expect to see us again? That we should have been frightened away by now?

"I was hoping you might be able to help us. Maybe you know a little bit about Perdita, its history?"

"There's rumored to be a secret," Rose whispered, looking behind her.

"We've figured that much out," said Boges. "We've heard stories of a sunken ship . . . laden with treasure . . . "

The curtain that separated the shop from the residence billowed open and Curly stepped through the doorway. Rose shrank in fear.

"What have you been saying, woman?" He was trying to smile, to make it sound like a joke, but it wasn't. Behind the false grin, his eyes were hard. "Frightening the customers?"

"Nothing, dear. Just chatting . . . " Rose was Curly's wife?

"That's right," I said lightly. "We were just asking your wife about the history of the local area."

"I heard you asking about a secret and that old house," he said. "Something to do with a ship? Where'd you hear that?"

I flashed him my prettiest smile. "Places like that always have secrets. Plus, the house is built in the shape of a ship."

I could see that Curly wasn't convinced. He continued to look at me suspiciously. "The only mystery I can think of is why you want to stay there. There are some very nice rental properties closer to town—nice and modern, with big balconies, swimming pools and all that stuff that you young folk like. I could get you a very good discount."

"Thanks, Curly," said Boges, "but we're pretty happy where we are."

Curly looked hard at Boges. "What about some more cookies and cheese, Mrs. Curlewis? And some orange juice?" Boges continued.

Perdita

5:25 pm

"Curly is hiding something for sure," I said. "And it's obvious his wife is scared to death of him." We were standing in front of the fire, and I picked the Perdita file up off the top of the carved mantelpiece where I'd left it, intending to search it one more time for hidden secrets. As I did so, I took a long look at the mantelpiece itself. "You know, there's something about this carving," I said. "It seems out of place. Why is there an acorn sticking out of a gum tree design?"

I ran my fingers along the carvings, the graceful wattle flowers and gum leaves chiseled out of the dark wood. I felt around and then leaned on the acorn. The carving suddenly caved in under my fingers. "Oh no! I've broken it! I didn't mean to press so hard."

A creaking and knocking noise seemed to come from the nearby wall and I jumped back in fright.

"What's that?" Ryan cried.

"Watch out!" Boges yelled. "The whole wall is moving!"

The three of us gaped as the wood panel closest to the right-hand side of the fireplace slowly opened, revealing a dark space inside.

"I don't believe it! A secret room!" I gasped.

"How cool is that!" Boges said.

"What's in there?" asked Ryan, poking his head in and then pulling it out fast, tearing cobwebs away from his face. "Ugh! Spider webs!"

Boges found the flashlight and shone it into the hole. "It looks like a passageway," he reported.

"What are we waiting for?" I couldn't wait to get in there, spiders or not. "Come on, follow me." I grabbed the flashlight from Boges and stepped into the dark space, shining the light ahead of me.

The passage ran along to the left, behind the fireplace and along the wall of the front room, a narrow walkway hemmed in by solid walls. The others jostled behind me, heads down under the low ceiling. After about seven paces, the passage made a sharp turn to the right and I figured this must have been somewhere under the bedroom I'd been sleeping in. "There's a right-hand turn here, guys," I called back. I followed the passageway a short distance to where a narrow flight of steps started. Shining the flashlight on the dusty floor revealed the first of the steps . . . and something else. "Someone's been here recently," I said. "You can see the footprints in the dust."

"That would explain the knocking and scratching in the walls!" said Boges.

The steps were steep and narrow. I went up and up, and suddenly banged my head on a low ceiling. Hunched over, I shone the flashlight above me. I'd run into a dead end above my head.

"That looks like floorboards," said Boges. "Must be the room above us."

I switched off the flashlight and heard the others gasp behind me.

"What did you do that for?" asked Boges. "Want to give us all claustrophobia?"

Now that it was pitch-black, I could see a faint, square outline through which tiny chinks of light shone between the floorboards above me.

"There's a trapdoor here," I said, "just above my head." I switched the flashlight back on, and tried to push it up. "I can't budge it."

"Let me try," said Ryan. There was hardly any room for him to get past me and I was nearly crushed as he took my place.

"It's no use," he called back. "It must be locked. What room's on the other side of this?" Ryan asked.

"I don't know. It could be the room I've been sleeping in, that front bedroom."

"We've climbed higher than that," said Boges, "past that bedroom. I think it's that little lookout room above your bedroom, Winter."

"Of course!" I said, excited. "That's where they set up the video projector! They used the secret tunnel, crept up here and somehow knew how to open the trapdoor. There's only that old chest up there." I suddenly understood. "Come on!"

We turned around and made our way back to the opening next to the fireplace. We thundered upstairs to the lookout room. The three of us were about to move the heavy chest when I noticed something. "Look at the dust on the floor—you can see the outline of the chest just there, next to where it's standing on the rug now. Someone's moved it over the trapdoor."

We heaved the chest away, pulled back the rug and sure enough, right in the floorboards, was a trapdoor with a slide lock. It opened easily and as we peered in, we could see the steps leading down into the tunnel.

"So," said Boges, "the 'ghost' is finally laid to rest. Someone came through the secret passage, climbed up here with the projector, played the footage of the ghost onto the smoke and then left the same way. These steps go past the wall of your bedroom, Winter. No wonder you could hear strange noises in the night."

"They couldn't have pulled that chest across the trapdoor once they were underneath it," I pointed out, with a shiver. "They must have come down the main stairs behind us when we went outside to investigate."

"Man, that is spooky," said Boges.

"What is it about me?" I cried. "This is the second house where I've had intruders! And what about the Drowner? Don't forget that clock is ticking down, and we don't even know who it is!"

"Calm down, Winter," said Ryan, putting an arm around me. "No one's going to hurt you while I'm around." He looked and sounded so like Cal in that moment, I almost forgot that it was Ryan.

"Thanks," I said, stepping over to the window. A thought came to me. "What if this isn't the only secret tunnel?"

"Good point," said Boges, excited by the possibility. "There might be more in another direction. Let's go down and check it out."

6:32 pm

We climbed down through the trapdoor and followed the tunnel back to the entrance to the front room. We were almost at the end of the passageway and about to step out when I spotted something on the floor—something shiny. I bent down and scratched dirt away from it. It looked like a ring of some sort.

It was hard work in the squashed passageway,

but we took turns and eventually uncovered a heavy brass ring, attached to the ground.

"This is it," said Ryan, as he scraped the last of the dirt away to reveal a large slab of the rock. "Looks like we need to lift this whole stone up," he added.

This trapdoor proved much tougher than the first one and it was obvious that it hadn't been used in a very long time. Our arms strained levering the heavy stone up, but finally we managed to lift it right out. For the second time that evening, we were peering into the black unknown.

I shone the flashlight down. This time, stone steps carpeted in thick dust fell away steeply and vanished around a corner. "This one seems to go away from the house," I said, trying to discern more in the light.

7:01 pm

I lowered myself down onto the stone steps and into the narrow passageway. Slowly, I descended the stairs, Boges and Ryan close behind me. I heard Boges sneeze from the dust and Ryan almost slipped on a step, grabbing me to stop his fall. I took hold of his arm and for a moment we held each other until he regained his balance. "You OK?" I asked.

"Fine, Winter."

I lifted the flashlight to reveal a small stone room ahead of us.

"It's an old cellar," said Boges, switching on the light on his phone. Ryan did the same to reveal a small, damp square room that had been hewn out of the rock. The stillness was broken only by the swing and thud of the nearby ocean, a dim, intermittent roar. A huge iron hook on a thick iron chain hung from the cellar's roof and I wondered what it was for—maybe hanging meat or fish to dry out.

"In the old days, before refrigeration," Boges said, "people needed cool, dark places to keep their vegetables."

The light from my flashlight blinked and dimmed. "The batteries are dying," I said. "Let's get better equipment so that we can really explore. We need some good lighting."

"We really need some good food, too," said Boges. "I'm starving!"

"Me too," said Ryan. "C'mon, we'll make a fresh start in the morning."

I called Cal to give him an update.

"Secret passages? I wish I was there!"

"They'll still be here when you get here, don't worry," I laughed.

DAY 20

11 days to go . . .

Secret passageway, Perdita

8:34 am

The next morning, we couldn't wait to get back to exploring. We hurriedly put new batteries in my flashlight and found Ryan's camping light.

We made our way through the secret passage and down the stone steps to the cellar. It was mesmerizing to hear the sound of the sea so close, the shuddering dump of a wave as it struck the rocky beach beneath us. But there was something else. I strained to listen.

"Shh!" I hissed. "Quiet, everyone! I can hear something. What is that?"

We all stopped to listen.

"All I can hear is the sea, crashing on the rocks," said Ryan.

"Can't you hear voices? Or is it just one voice?"

"Winter, you are seriously freaking me out! What voice?"

"Shut up, Boges," I ordered, "and just listen."

"Hey! You're right. I can hear it too," said Ryan.

"But where is it coming from?" asked Boges. "Outside somewhere? It doesn't sound like it's upstairs."

"Amazing that the sound penetrates down here," I said. "But I can't make out any words."

"Let's go take a look," said Ryan.

We retraced our steps back into the house, and climbed straight up to the lookout room overlooking the sea, trying to get a fix on where the voice might have come from.

I looked out the window and immediately noticed someone moving around near the back of Perdita. The person came fully into view. "Curly is snooping around down there! What's he up to now?"

"Let's find out," Boges said.

"Don't let him out of your sight," I hissed, as we hurried down the front hall. We watched as Curly headed for the bush track that led to the beach.

We followed and peered over the edge of the cliff to see Curly making his way down the steps. We watched him all the way down until he reached the sand. Then he seemed to be poking around with a long stick that he'd picked up.

"He's looking for something," I said, "in the rocks down there."

"Let's get down there and check out what he's up to," said Ryan.

It wasn't so hard getting down the cliff this time, and although I was worried that Curly might look up and see us coming, there didn't seem to be much danger of that. He was completely absorbed in what he was doing—looking around the big boulders that were strewn along the base of the cliff.

Finally, the three of us landed quietly on the beach some distance away from Curly, whose stooped figure was still probing and prodding between the rocks. Cautiously, we approached, keeping low and some distance behind him.

"Don't move," I whispered to the others. "He's calling someone on his phone."

"We need to listen in," Boges pointed out.

"You're right. But I think only one of us should get closer—less chance of being spotted. I'll go," I volunteered. "You two stay here."

Crouching down, I crept closer until I found a large boulder and ducked behind it. I had a good line of sight to Curly, who was sitting on a rock not far from me, talking loudly on his phone. I turned and beckoned to the other two and they snuck over to join me.

"People have already died trying to find it," we heard Curly say. "I don't want to be next." There was a long pause as he listened. Then, "It's supposed to be somewhere here, but I can't find it. It's just a pile of rocks."

Boges nudged me. "That was the voice we could hear in the cellar," he hissed. "It must have been Curly." Boges's voice fell silent as Curly's voice continued, "What am I supposed to do about it?" he asked the unknown caller. "They're all here and they're not leaving."

The person on the other end must have said something that annoyed Curly because he angrily shoved his phone in his pocket, stood up and started to stride away, turning in our direction while we flattened ourselves on the sand behind the boulder.

He walked straight past us only a small distance away, head down, muttering. Yet all the time, those hard eyes were scanning the beach.

I nudged Boges. "Let's find where he hangs out when he's not scaring his wife in the shop."

Keeping well back, we set out to follow him, all the way along the beach.

"People have died trying to find—what?" Boges asked. "Was he talking about the shipwreck? Is it supposed to be somewhere here near these rocks?"

"I don't know," I said, keeping an eye on the distant figure at the other end of the beach and hastening my steps. "But we mustn't lose him."

"He's been watching us the whole time and he doesn't like that we're still here. Because we're in the way," Ryan said.

"It's pretty obvious," said Boges, "that he's working for whoever he was talking to. Curly is only an employee."

"Hey, look!" I said as we came around a bend. "He's heading up the hill to that house way over there."

We stood and watched as Curly disappeared into a modern glass and concrete mansion. It stood by itself in a commanding position on the northern headland of Deception Bay, facing out to sea.

"So the question is, who lives there?" I said.

9:07 am

Following carefully behind, we made our way up until we were hiding in the bushland that surrounded the mansion.

I edged closer, keeping some cover between me and the house. Luckily, we were approaching from the side, away from the road to the village out in front. There was nowhere to hide on the neat lawns between us and the house.

"Check out the security cameras," said Boges, pointing to the small black boxes on each corner of the building. "This is high-grade security."

As we watched, one of the garage double-doors slowly started rising and we strained to see who might be driving the red sports car backing out. But once out of the garage, the driver gunned the motor and screeched off down the side of the building and onto the road, too fast for me to get much more than a fleeting glimpse. They took off towards the village in a cloud of dust.

"Same driving school as Harriet," chuckled Ryan to himself.

"Did you get to see who it was?" I asked.

"Too quick for me. But I'm betting it wasn't Curly," said Ryan.

"Let's take a closer look at the house," Boges said.

Staying down, the three of us ran over to the garage, now closed again. Pressed against the wall, I sidled up to a window and peered through.

It was a living room, with a few magazines piled on a table, comfortable chairs and a bright-purple rug on the floor. Everything was quiet and still. But in a mirror on the far wall, I saw the reflection of a woman with short, spiky hair, her back to us, in the adjoining room, sitting at a desk.

I was staring at this reflection when a door

flew open with a bang and I nearly died of fright as a huge Doberman came bounding through. I bolted. I barely saw the man who was racing after the dog.

"Hey, you little punks! Get off this property! What do you think you're doing here?"

Over the sound of the dog's furious barking, I could hear the pounding of Boges's and Ryan's feet behind me as we crashed into the bushland.

"Split up!" Boges yelled, and we did—with me racing straight ahead, Boges and Ryan peeling off to the left and right.

Branches and sharp twigs tore at my face and arms, snagging my hair, but I kept running and finally the sound of the dog's barking started fading. I saw the boys ahead of me and raced up to join them, where we caught our breath.

"I think I just lost ten years off my life," said Boges, doubled over and panting. "That dog was the last thing I was expecting."

Just as he was catching his breath again, his phone rang. He slowed his breathing as he answered. "What is it, Mum?" he asked. Then I saw his face flicker with concern. "Sure," he said. "I'll leave right away. I should be back in a few hours, OK?" He hung up.

"What is it, Boges?" Ryan asked.

"It's Gran. She's had to go to the hospital. Mum

needs me. I'm sorry, guys, I'll have to go back to the city."

"That's too bad," said Ryan, "on both counts."

"I hope your gran's OK," I said.

"I hate to go—" Boges began, but I took his arm.

"You've got to go, no question, Boges," I said. "Family is so important. Your mum needs you."

"It's only for a day or two," said Boges. "Mum's not really good at filling out official forms—she finds the language difficult sometimes. Plus she'll need me to drive her around."

Back at Perdita, I considered my options. Even though it was important that we discover who lived in that mansion, it wouldn't hurt to take a couple of days off. And it would be unthinkable to mount a surveillance operation on the place without Boges.

"How about we take a break, too, Ryan?" I said. "This is a good chance to go back home, have a decent hot shower, get some takeout and take stock of everything that's happened so far. I should probably work on my vacation assignment, too."

We drove back to the city, Boges dropping off Ryan first and then me. "Give my love to your gran," I said as he left.

DAY 22

9 days to go . . .

Home
Mansfield Way, Dolphin Point

8:03 pm

I spent the next two days dealing with the mail that had arrived while I'd been away at Perdita and calling Boges to see how his gran was doing. Cal called too.

"What's been happening? Any more ghosts?" he laughed.

I brought him up to date. "I can't wait to get back down there," I said, "and find out what Curly was looking for. And it'd be good to check out that house on the headland again."

"I'll be done here next weekend," said Cal. "I might even be able to leave earlier after we have the final course exams next week. I'll spend a night with Mum and Gabbi on the way, and then I'll ride down to Perdita."

"Can't wait," I said.

DAY 26

5 days to go . . .

Perdita

10:09 am

The previous evening, with Boges's gran on the mend, the three of us had driven back down to Perdita. It was good to be back in the big front room again with a fire blazing. Perdita no longer felt strange to me.

The next morning, we made our way down to the beach. Ryan had brought his climbing gear in case we felt like trying it out. The sun was warm, although a strong wind blew in from the sea. We sat on the rocks at the base of the cliff, planning our next move. "Last time we were here," I told the others, "I saw that woman at the house on the headland—the one with really short hair. But we still don't know who she is."

"She's got some overkill security," said Boges, "which really makes me suspicious."

"Maybe she's just nervous," said Ryan, "living alone."

"But she's not alone," Boges said. "A guy was driving that car, and another set the dog after us."

"And why was Curly sniffing around down here?" I said. "I'd love to know what he was looking for." I was eager to take action, so I climbed over the large boulders behind us, piled up like huge building blocks. As I straightened up, looking back at the way we'd come down, I looked at the cliff looming before me and noticed a small overhang just above the pile of rocks on the beach.

"Boges! Ryan! Come here! See, next to that old fence post? I want to go up there and take a look." I clambered over the rocks and a little way up the cliff, stepping onto protruding stones some distance away from the cliff path.

"Glad I brought all this gear," Ryan complained. "What a waste. Hope you don't fall and break a leg!"

In less than a minute, I was at the overhang, holding on to the iron post, once part of a now-derelict fence. Why was there a fence in this strange position? I pushed away hanging vines and weeds. I could hear a churning noise, a whooshing. Curious, I stooped to get in under the overhang, not much bigger than a beach shelter.

There, in the back wall, was a narrow cleft. I squeezed through it and gasped.

I had stepped into another world!

11:35 am

I was standing on a small rocky ledge in a large cave, where six feet beneath me, the turquoise sea frothed and crashed, racing around the cave and vanishing into several dark, echoing openings. I stood there transfixed by the beauty, unaware that Ryan and Boges had squeezed through and were standing beside me.

"Awesome!" Ryan breathed. "What an unreal place!"

Beneath us, the sea sucked and swirled, forced through the narrow entrance by the power of the massive ocean swells, lit underneath by the magic light coming through the cracks in the rocks from the beach, and rushing up to disappear down three dark arches.

"Look, there are a few tunnels going back under the cliff," I said. "I wonder if there are more caves. A rock fall must have blocked off the main entrance and now only the sea can force its way through. This is the only way in, through this little overhang."

"So that's what Curly is looking for," said Ryan. "A way into these caves. But why would he be interested in them? No ship could get in here in the first place!"

"When we get a warmer day," I said, "we should go sea caving. We'll need ropes and waterproof lights."

"I've got ropes," Ryan said. "And we'll need to watch the tide, too. It's coming in now, you can tell."

It was true. Even in the short time we'd been on the ledge, it was clear that each wave was washing in a little higher than the one before. I looked around for a tidemark to see how far the water rose inside. Boges must have been reading my mind because I saw him pointing across the cave to the opposite wall.

"There's the high-water mark," he said. "The water will be up to this ledge that we're standing on then."

"Cool," said Ryan. "We can jump into the water from here."

"And it's probably easier to swim through the system," Boges said, "than try to scramble over the rocky floors and walls. This will be a great spot in the summer!"

As we climbed back up the cliff, we made plans as to what to do next. Ryan volunteered to lead the expedition.

"We need the right gear," he said, "and to be roped together . . . and we'll need good lighting."

"While you sort that out, we'll find out who's behind Curly—who's really pulling the strings," Boges said. "That mansion needs surveillance."

"I'm not keen on becoming a Doberman's breakfast," I said.

"Remote surveillance, Winter," said Boges. "You couldn't have forgotten my Humming-bird Hawk-moth creation already?" Boges had adapted a couple of tiny drones—flying spy cameras—which had been very helpful when we'd found ourselves up against Sligo once more.

"I'm going to modify one," he said, "and send it on a fact-finding mission. Just give me a day to organize it. And we should go into the village and see what intel we can get from the locals about this place and that shipwreck."

As we approached the house, I couldn't help glancing over at the grove, with its forbidding cypress trees crowded together. I was determined to hack a way through that dense, green-black wall and uncover the building hidden at its heart.

DAY 27

4 days to go . . .

Perdita

3:45 am

I bolted awake! What time was it? I grabbed my phone from beside my bed. It was still so early, but something had woken me from a deep sleep. I sat up, straining to listen. Silently, I crept over to the half-closed French doors to the balcony and looked out. It was pitch-black outside and I nearly screamed as someone crashed into me in the dark.

"Shh!" whispered Boges. "It's me. Sorry, I can't see a thing. Did you hear that? Someone's in the secret passageway!"

I picked up my flashlight, switching it on. "Right. This time we're going to nab him. Get Ryan."

"I'm already here," Ryan whispered loudly from the darkened doorway.

Again came the scratching and knocking that I'd heard in the walls two weeks ago when the "ghost" first put in an appearance.

"I can't wait to get my hands on whoever's been trying to scare me out of my own house. This time, they won't get away with it."

We crept down the main staircase, not really needing the flashlight, knowing our way through the darkness now, pausing outside the door to the big front room. I briefly shone the flashlight beam in front of me. On the floor near the entrance lay the old sheet that Ryan had used to scare us on that first night at Perdita and I picked it up.

I whispered instructions. "We'll wait at the entrance to the passageway and as soon as he starts coming through the doorway into the room, we throw this over him and take him down. Ryan—you grab his legs, Boges—you sit on him and pin his arms. I'll be on standby with the flashlight, ready to whack him if he gives us any trouble, OK?"

"Got it," whispered Ryan.

We tiptoed into the room and another quick beam from the flashlight showed that the secret panel was open, revealing a darker blackness within.

We positioned ourselves silently—the boys on either side of the passage doorway, me a little to one side with the old sheet in one hand and my heavy flashlight raised in the other, ready for action.

The knocking and scratching became louder and now we could hear whispers and muttering.

Maybe he was having some difficulty finding his way out. So much the better, I thought. He'll be disoriented and completely taken by surprise by our ambush.

My mouth was dry with excitement and I could hear my heart banging in my chest. The enemy came closer, the sounds drew nearer, then finally, like a grub coming out of a hole, a head, upper body and then lower body emerged.

"Get him!" I yelled, throwing the sheet over the intruder. The boys moved like lightning, crash-tackling him down to the floor, where he floundered and kicked and yelled . . .

That voice!

It couldn't be!

"Better watch out! Black belt! Black belt! You let me go right now! Nearly won the karate championship in Hong Kong! Let me up if you know what's good for you!"

I dragged the sheet off the struggling figure and shone my flashlight on his face.

"*Repro?*"

Boges and Ryan stared as the skinny figure clambered to his feet, brushing himself and his tattered bag down.

"What sort of welcome is *that*? I come all the way from the city to give you a hand, and you treat me like this? There's no justice in the world—that's what I told the magistrate."

I don't know who was more shocked—Repro or us, as he stood there in his old green coat with the too-short sleeves, green fingerless mittens on his long hands, a moth-eaten beanie on his head, and a green-and-red scarf around his scrawny neck, now covered in dust. Cal and I had outfitted him with a brand-new wardrobe, but obviously Repro was happier in his preferred style, although he seemed to have put on a bit of weight.

"You've gotten a bit heavier," I said, pointing to him. He looked quite plump.

"Nah," he said. "It's my layers. I'm wearing all my clothes. Saves packing them."

"What on earth are you doing here?" I asked, adding hastily, "I mean, it's great to see you. But what are you doing in the secret passage?"

"What are you doing attacking me with high tackles? Secret passage? I thought this was a regular doorway. I was trying to get upstairs."

We burst out laughing, the three of us shaking with relieved tension and hilarity while Repro glowered in the middle.

"How did you get into the house?" Ryan asked.

"There was a very convenient lock on the front door, through which I was able to effect entry," Repro said in a snooty voice.

"You mean you picked the lock," said Boges.

I took Repro's arm and then hugged him. "It's so good to see you, Repro," I said. But a thought struck me. "You mean the entrance to the secret passage was open?"

"Of course it was. Even I can't walk through walls!"

"I didn't open it," said Boges.

"Me neither," added Ryan.

I knew I hadn't.

"Well, someone's been here, during the night," Boges said, "before Repro blundered in."

"Excuse me, I don't blunder," Repro corrected. "I'm very nimble on my feet, thank you."

"OK, twinkle toes," I said, "how about a hot chocolate?"

4:31 am

We sat around the rebuilt fire, and between the three of us, brought Repro up to speed on what had been going on at Perdita and what we'd discovered so far. We discussed who might have been snooping in the secret passage.

"It must be someone who knows the house," I said. "Someone who knows the history of this place." I thought of Harriet immediately, but dismissed the idea. Why would she be poking around in here?

As if reading my mind, Boges said, "Harriet seems to know more than she's saying. It's possible she knows about the secret passage."

"But why on earth would she be creeping around in there in the middle of the night?" I asked.

"Same reason as anybody else," said Ryan. "To discover the secret of Perdita—that's why. If she found the treasure, her money problems would be solved."

I told Repro about Harriet and her dried-up farm, then about the mansion on the northern headland, the woman with the spiky hair and the security guard with the Doberman.

"Interesting that Curly was able to just walk straight into that house, without knocking. The Doberman didn't go for him, did it?" Boges pointed out.

"Horrible hounds," said Repro. "Had a run-in once with one of those." Repro took it all in, demolishing a package of chocolate cookies and drinking several cups of tea in quick succession.

"So how did you know where we were?" I asked.

"Cal called me from flight school. He thought you might need a hand down here. I couldn't come earlier because I've been—err—taking a break from society for a while. Doing some meditation."

"Don't tell me you've been to a retreat? A

health spa, perhaps?" asked Ryan.

"More like a strict health farm," said Repro. "I overlooked a few fines from the constabulary."

"How many?" Boges asked.

"Not quite sure," said Repro cagily. "More than a few. And the constabulary took a dim view. All I did was camp in some places they didn't think I should be in and I failed 'to move along when required.' I wasn't doing any harm."

"But why were you camping out?" I asked, puzzled. "You've got a beautiful house of your own now. And what about your mum?"

"I have a gypsy soul, my girl," said Repro grandly. "And I miss my underground home—all those exciting tunnels, my underground lake, my plans for my Underland Wonderland resort. My mum wants me to join the local lawn bowling club. Wear those white bowling trousers and sweaters, and a canvas hat," he shuddered. "My house is very nice, and I don't mean to be ungrateful to you and young Cal, but it's just not me. Everyone knows where I live now. I even get *mail!*"

"Mail! How terrible!" I joked.

Repro didn't miss a beat. "So I followed my gypsy soul."

"And that led you where, exactly?" asked Boges.

"Various places," he said vaguely, "which in turn led to the non-payment of a number of fines.

I could either pay up or spend a week at one of Her Majesty's correctional institutions. I chose to be detained," Repro said,

"You mean you were in jail?" said Ryan.

Repro sniffed and refused to answer, instead looking around for more chocolate cookies.

"I'm going back to bed," I announced. "Repro, that big armchair near the fire is very comfortable. I'll bring you a blanket. We'll figure out a plan in the morning. And there's something I want to show you, too."

10:40 am

After a breakfast of toast and eggs, we cleaned up and found that Repro had pieced together a lot of the jigsaw puzzle on the floor during the early hours of the morning. Now we could see that it was shaping up to be some kind of building surrounded by gardens.

From the folder in my bag, I pulled out the strange and menacing newspaper clipping I'd been sent weeks ago, passing it to Repro.

"What do you make of this, Repro?" I asked. He studied it, his shrewd, bright eyes scanning the typed script and the two scribbled words, *The Drowner . . . 30 days.*

Eventually, he handed it back to me, shaking his head. "Can't help you with that, Winter.

Where did it come from?"

I told him. "I'm not sure whether it's a threat, or a warning. Either way, it's completely useless, until we know who the Drowner is."

"Sounds like a person," said Repro, "and someone I wouldn't like to meet—especially near water," said Repro.

"Plenty of that around here," said Ryan. "Actually, we've been thinking all this time that it came from someone in the city, but maybe it's a threat from somebody here who knows about the Perdita file and this house. It might be just another attempt to frighten us away. There are only four days left until the deadline—surely if it was something dangerous, we'd know by now."

"It all started with this," I said, picking up the Perdita file.

Repro flicked through it. "And what's this?" he asked, noticing the envelope stuck at the back and taking out the paper with the strange drawing.

"We don't know," I said. "We all thought it looked a bit like a ghost." I pointed out the strange shapes. "But now I'm inclined to think it's just a scribble."

Repro peered more closely at the old piece of paper, scrutinizing it thoroughly.

"Mmm," he muttered. "It reminds me of something. Something I saw a magician do. If you look closely, you can see fold lines in the paper—I don't mean all the wrinkled, crumpled bits—I mean these straight lines here, where it's been folded and unfolded a lot." With a few deft movements, Repro folded the paper a couple of times and something happened. The lines now connected up, creating one shape.

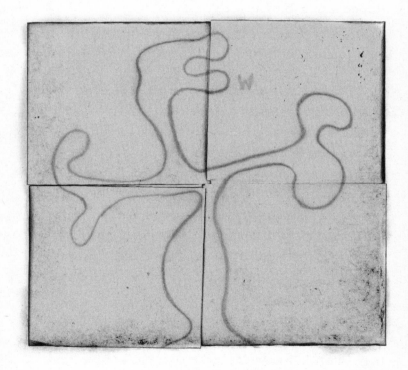

"That's amazing!" I said. "Now it looks more like a piece of coral, with branches on it. Somebody wanted to hide this drawing," I said. "Why?"

Another one of Perdita's secrets was staring us in the face, taunting us.

"Coral, you said?" said Repro, with the beginning of a grin. "Did I ever tell you that I lived in some speleological structures for a while?"

"Some *whats*?" Ryan asked.

"He means caves," said Boges, puncturing Repro's overblown language.

"Yes, well," I said, "you've lived in some very unusual places. But why are you telling us this now?"

"There must be caves around here, that's why. This reminds me of a cave system."

"The sea caves!" I cried. "That's what it is! It's a diagram of the layout of the caves!"

Boges grabbed the diagram from Repro. "Yes! The caves that Curly is looking for! And he doesn't know the way in—but we do!"

The thrill of discovery bubbled through my veins. We'd unlocked another of Perdita's secrets.

"And look," Boges added, "we were looking at it upside down before. That's not an M—it's a W."

"Windraker!" I yelled. "Is that where the Windraker is lying? That's what Curly and his boss want! But we're going to get there first!" I was jumping out of my skin with excitement. I couldn't wait to start exploring the cave system.

"I doubt it, Winter," Boges said, shaking his

head. "No ship could fit in through the narrow entry to the caves."

"Hang on! What's a Windraker?" asked Repro, looking bewildered. "Have I missed something?"

We quickly filled Repro in on everything we'd heard about the shipwreck that lay somewhere in Deception Bay.

"Whatever is hidden in the caves," Boges said, "it must be very important. Otherwise why would someone hide it with that fancy folding-paper trick? And whatever it is, it's hidden right at the very back of the furthest and biggest cave."

Sea caves system

1:26 pm

One by one, the three of us squeezed through the narrow cleft hidden by the overhang of the cliff, carrying our gear. Repro had chosen to stay behind, allegedly to guard Perdita from any further intruders.

Boges had helped Ryan make waterproof lights by sealing our flashlights in tall, airtight jam jars with ropes attached to them.

"They'll float, too," Ryan said, "so we won't lose them. I'll get real waterproof lights just as soon as I can."

It was cold inside the cave and the water swirled

underneath the rocky ledge. Chinks of light shone like tiny spotlights onto the roiling water. I angled my jar flashlight hanging from my neck to light up the back of the cave and revealed the three smaller tunnels leading down into unknown darkness. Boges had the folded diagram protected in a plastic sheet. "Whatever we're looking for," he said, jabbing at the diagram in the light, "is right at the back of the far cave, through that middle tunnel. Who's game enough to go first?"

"Me!" Ryan and I yelled together, then laughed, the sound of which echoed through the underground caverns. I jumped in, Ryan right behind me and Boges bringing up the rear. The water was freezing and deeper than I expected, and I couldn't touch the bottom. I squealed and again the sound bounced around the walls of the caves.

Away from the boulder-blocked main entrance, it was very dark and only the beams from our jar-lights penetrated, illuminating the rocky walls and making the low ceilings of the middle tunnel glisten. It was easy swimming. Small crabs scuttled up the walls and shiny black sea snails clustered in groups. One day, I thought, we would explore the whole system.

The current was stronger where the water was being forced into the narrower channel, pushing us through until we came up into the middle cave.

Our flashlights bobbed along on the currents in their watertight jars, throwing light onto star-fish and tiny sea creatures. We swam through and into a wide cave, assisted by the current.

"Oh wow!" I said, as I trod water and directed my light around a round cavern the size of a tennis court. The boys came splashing in behind me and the domed roof lit up with their extra lights. The ceiling dripped with stalactites of strange sea plants and pale crustaceans scurried into their hiding places.

We found that the cold water was only frac-tionally warmer than the freezing air of the cavern. I looked across at Boges and Ryan, their teeth chattering in their heads just like mine. My fingertips ached with the cold.

We searched all around the alcove marked with the W, and although I hadn't really been expecting to find a shipwreck just sitting in the cave, it seemed like there was nothing there at all, except the sea creatures.

We turned our attention to the stunning roof of the cavern and I gasped as we all saw it together. We focused our lights on something wedged firmly into a cavity high up on the back wall of the alcove, right up near the ceiling. We swam closer, peering up to try to see what it was.

"It looks like an old strongbox—you know,

those old metal boxes with locks that people used to keep valuables in," said Boges.

"Looks like it's been pushed into a crevice. If Captain Greenlowe put that in position a hundred years ago and it's still there," I said, "my bet is that it's very firmly wedged in." In spite of the freezing water, and my chattering teeth, thrilling excitement was coursing through my blood. Everything we'd done so far had worked towards this exhilarating moment. I realized I was kicking my legs underwater in crazy excitement, like a little kid. There was something else too, above the crevice where the metal box was wedged—it looked like someone had carved a square into the rock that formed the roof of this huge cave.

"There's no way we can get up there," said Ryan, who had been swimming around, trying to find a way to approach the wall. "It's way out of our reach. You'd have to be Spiderman to get up there."

"There's got to be a way. How else did Captain Greenlowe manage to get it up there in the first place?" I asked. The frustration was crushing. *We'll never find out the truth*, I thought, my spirits dampened.

12:02 pm

Brain churning desperately, I directed my flashlight around the walls of the cave, trying to find some handhold, some way to get up to where the box was wedged.

That's when I noticed a very clear high-water mark, about three feet beneath the crevice holding the tantalizing box.

"Of course!" I cried, swinging my flashlight all around the circular walls of the big cavern. "We just have to come here at high tide! We'll probably have to swim underwater through the tunnel to get into this big cave. That way, when we surface, we'll be really close to the crevice. I bet if we bring the right tools, we'll be able to dislodge that box!"

"Totally! That's perfect, Winter!" said Boges. "I just wonder if we can do it in one breath? I guess we can only try."

"Although there's still a gap between the high-water mark and the box," Ryan added. "I wonder how someone got it up there? Maybe we need to wait for a really strong tide to get close enough."

"We can do that," I agreed. We took a few more minutes to explore the big cave, but I could tell the boys were as eager as I was to plan our second visit to uncover this underwater secret as soon as possible.

DAY 28

3 days to go . . .

Perdita

8:33 am

The next morning, we were busy figuring out our next adventure to the sea caves system. The old house was buzzing with excitement and I had stunned Repro by grabbing him and dancing with him around the room.

Boges had searched online for the high tide information and had downloaded a chart for the next few days.

"Great," I said, "that's done. We'll wait for a day with bigger swells, then go in at high tide, surface nice and close to where that box is wedged, and work on it until we free it. Then we bring it home and see what we've got. I can hardly wait!"

"It might be full of gold," said Ryan, "or jewels."

"Could be," said Boges. "I bet it's more likely to be a treasure map."

"But, Boges," I said, worried now, "if it's a map, wouldn't it be rotted by now?"

"The old charts were all on vellum—like the Ormond Riddle. Vellum lasts for ages. And the metal box is above the high-water mark."

"If it's the map leading to the Windraker," said Ryan, jiggling with excitement, "we'll be able to find the shipwreck!"

A noise outside the front door made all of us swing around.

"What was that?" I asked.

"Someone's here! I can hear them running away. Come on!" said Ryan, racing outside.

We fanned out in all different directions, but I soon slowed, and then stopped. I noticed that the others had too. It was no use. The spy had escaped.

"He could have heard everything about the sea caves and the Windraker," said Boges.

"What if it's a she, not a he?" Ryan asked. "I'm just saying it's possible."

I remained silent. I really didn't want to think of Harriet as someone who snooped around, eavesdropping. If she turned out to be an enemy, I'd be hurt as well as angry. "We've still got the advantage of knowing how to get into the sea caves," I said. "No one else knows that and they don't know exactly where the metal box is. It's going to take anyone else a while to figure all that out. We're still ahead of the game. And anyway, we can't go until the tide is right."

"There's something else I want to do," said Boges. "I'm launching Skyshadow over that mansion so we can keep an eye on movements along the coast," Boges said, bringing out his new device.

We crowded around to see what Boges had made. He'd adapted a novelty seagull toy to house a mini-camera. Both the tiny motor and the camera were powered by batteries. "This will send back a live feed to my computer for at least two hours," he explained. "We might get an idea of what's going on there and a better look at punk woman."

"Skyshadow?" Repro asked. "I could use something like that." Repro was keen to come with us as we went to the edge of the cliff to watch the launch. The bird took off beautifully, propeller spinning invisibly, and soared up and away while Boges steered it with the remote joystick.

A few moments later, and it was indistinguishable—just another bird almost out of sight, like the dozens of others that swirled around the beach.

"I'll stay here," said Boges, "and keep an eye on that house."

"Come on, guys," I said to Ryan and Repro, "we're running out of food. Let's go into town and ask a few more questions. Boges, can I borrow your truck? I drive better than you anyway," I laughed.

Abercrombie Village

10:42 am

I headed into the village with Repro—Ryan had decided to stay back and continue clearing out more of the grove.

The little township was quiet at this mid-morning time, just a few people shopping, cars parked along the edge of the road, kids running around free from school on vacation. I headed straight for the general store. I was sure Rose could tell us a lot more. Repro stepped ahead of me at the doorway, gallantly holding back the plastic strips that kept the flies out of the shop so that I could walk through.

Rose looked up from her weather charts and a shy smile lit up her face.

"Good morning, Rose," I said, looking at some highly polished apples piled in a basket on the counter. "I'll take six of those, thanks," I said, pointing to them. Then I lowered my voice. "Rose, I need your help. Can you tell me anything you might know about the Windraker? I got the feeling you were going to tell us something last time before we were interrupted."

Rose's face paled. *Wrong question, Winter*, I scolded myself. But as I was kicking myself for scaring Rose, Repro had leaned an elbow on the counter as if he owned the place, winked at Rose in what he must have thought was a most alluring manner and asked, "Can you tell us anything you know, ma'am? Anything you might know about that old house, Perdita, and ghosts and secret passages? Any local knowledge about shipwrecked treasure?"

I kicked him hard on the ankle, frowning fiercely, my eyes messaging *Shut up, Repro*, as a slight movement of the curtain behind Rose alerted me to the fact that someone was there . . . again.

"What was that for?" he asked, looking very hurt.

I did my best to cover up Repro's words. "My friend is talking about a comic book he's reading. It's full of secret tunnels and ghosts and pirates and things."

"I am not! I don't read comics—" I kicked him again, really hard this time. Repro got it. "Oh, *that* comic? The one about the pirates?"

But it was too late.

No one came out from behind the curtain—

instead, I got the sense of a fleeting figure behind it, and heard a door slamming in the back somewhere.

I grabbed Repro firmly and dragged him, protesting loudly, out of the shop.

"Just sit here," I said, squashing him down on a bus stop bench near the shop. "Don't move and don't say a word to anyone until I get back."

I paid no attention to his muttering, "Bossy boots woman . . . pushing a fellow around." I ran as fast as I could, around the corner, desperate to see who had run out of the back of the shop. But when I reached the end of the alley and the back of the shop, no one was there, just the back gate swinging on its hinges. Whoever had been listening to us had vanished. Then from somewhere ahead of me, I heard the sound of a powerful car engine revving up and screeching off.

Then this too, faded into the distance. I immediately thought of the gas-head in the red sports car. Disappointed and still angry with Repro, I stomped back to the bus stop, to find him sitting there, dejected, and fiddling with his red-and-green scarf.

"I didn't know," he tried to explain. "I thought I was being helpful. Putting her at ease, so that she'd open up."

"Come on, let's go get those apples," I said, "and some more sausages. And some fresh bread."

When we went back inside, Rose's manner was very different. This time, there was no smile and she avoided eye contact as she got the supplies. She looked scared, shrunken. No way was she going to say a word about any secrets today. I paid and we left.

We pulled up outside Perdita and Ryan showed us where he'd started to clear a path through the grove.

"Great progress," I said. "Better than us. We didn't do much good in town. But I've got sausages for lunch."

"Cool. I'm going to keep going out here, so call me when they're cooked. And Boges is back, too."

Perdita

1:05 pm

As we came into the house, Boges was downstairs like a shot from the lookout room.

"Prepare yourself for a shock," said Boges. "I've got some good news and some bad news. First, the good news. Mission accomplished. Skyshadow is safely home. Come upstairs and have a look. Bad news, we are in big trouble."

"What is it, Boges?" I asked, now very alarmed.

"Just come up to the lookout room and you'll see what I mean."

Repro and I followed Boges up to the third floor, and peered at the screen of the laptop, seeing the aerial view that Skyshadow had sent back.

"Spit it out, Boges," I said. He paused for dramatic effect.

"I've ID'd the woman in the mansion."

"You know her?"

"I wish I didn't. Take a look."

Boges clicked on a new screen and the face of the spiky-haired woman appeared in grainy low resolution. But it was unmistakable. I gasped. *"Oriana de la Force!* That's who we're up against?" I stood there with my mouth open. Finally I was able to mumble, "She's supposed to be in jail!"

"That's what I thought. But I did some research. She's been released pending a judicial inquiry into her case. She's alleging that she's the victim of a mistrial. It's all there on my computer. You can read it for yourself."

I slid down the wall to the floor. "So she's behind all this. She must have been employing Curly—and that other person, the driver of the sports car, whoever that is. Plus security guy. Somehow, she's found out about the shipwreck."

"She was on to the mystery of the Ormond

Singularity way before we were," said Boges. "She's got her ways of sniffing out money."

"Boges, I'll bet she was the one who organized the private detective to break into my place. I couldn't read the signature on that check when we searched his office, but I remember thinking then that there was something familiar about the handwriting. Oriana organized to steal the Perdita file. She's never forgiven us for beating her to the Ormond Singularity and she blames us for the fact that she ended up in prison. Not to mention the indelible cat's whiskers drawn on her cheeks, although that really wasn't our fault. I doubt she cares! We need to be very careful. Oh no, do you think she could have sent the Drowner note? It would be just like her to do something like that to put us off the scent! She wanted Cal dead. We have to warn him. I'll call him now."

"Do you think that's a good idea?" Boges asked. "It'll only make him worry like crazy. He won't be able to do anything and he can't leave that residential school without blowing the whole course. He needs to be calm for the exams."

Boges had a point. "I guess we can handle this," I said, "but I should call Cal—he'll be wondering why I haven't."

"That woman. She's gotten worse since she's been in prison. I'll bet she's learned some very crooked new skills inside," Repro said. Then he noticed the heavy old chest near where I was sitting on the floor. "That's a very nice piece of cedar," he said. "What's inside it?"

"The jigsaw was in one drawer," I said. "Don't know what else is in there. The bottom drawer's jammed."

"These fancy fingers of mine," said Repro, flexing his skinny digits in the green mittens, "don't know the meaning of the words 'jammed' or 'locked.' Let's take a look." Repro examined the stuck drawer from every angle, muttering to himself. Finally, he spoke. "It's been pushed in incorrectly," he announced. "You can see that uneven angle across the top."

He disappeared downstairs for a moment, and returned bringing his old bag with him, selecting some of his locksmith tools. He did a little filing and poking around with a fine chisel and within minutes, the stuck drawer was free.

"What's this?" he said, lifting out an old book. Its cover had been water-damaged and it curled back, revealing damage to the interior pages.

"It's a photo album," I said, taking it from him, wrinkling my nose at the smell of rotting paper and damp. Sadly, it was almost totally destroyed and fell into useless lumps. But one page at the back of the album was still intact.

The picture was a very old sepia portrait of a beautiful young woman with a high collar, tiny seed pearl earrings, and her hair pinned up. "*Perdita Blanche Greenlowe, aged nineteen*," I read on the back.

It was very precious to have a picture of Captain Greenlowe's tragic young daughter. In spite of my really good friends, my deep friendships with Cal, Boges, and lately, Ryan, there was still an ache in my heart for family. Even though it was just a house, I felt a strong connection to Perdita, and having a picture of its namesake was amazing. I didn't know whether to cry with grief for her, or jump up and down with happiness at finding it. I felt someone slip an arm around me, and looked up, surprised. Ryan.

"I came inside to see what had happened to the sausages," he said, "and then realized everybody was up here. I know you're sad, Winter," he said, "but this picture is a really beautiful gift. One of this old house's good secrets."

I thanked Repro for opening the jammed drawer. Carefully, I took the old photograph and propped it up in my bedroom near the French doors.

I called Cal. I told him about finding the photograph, and about Repro's visit and how he had figured out the secret to the sea caves map and that he was now working hard on the jigsaw puzzle. I brought him up-to-date with almost everything, except the fact that his old enemy, Oriana de la Force, was only a relatively short distance away, and up to no good again.

Soon it was Cal's turn. "They've kept us insanely busy here," he said. "I've been working from about seven in the morning to eight at night, as well as flying five times a week. I'm cramming now for the test tomorrow morning." Just before he hung up, he asked, "Winter, are you OK? You'd tell me if there was something wrong—you promised, remember?"

"Of course," I said quickly. "Good luck in the exams and I'll see you soon."

DAY 29

2 days to go . . .

Perdita

9:55 am

It had been raining since the early hours, so we built up the fire to warm ourselves. Repro seemed to be devoting most of his time to the jigsaw puzzle. I went over to check it out. What I saw surprised and pleased me. "Hey!" I said. "It's a picture of Perdita, from when the house was in its heyday. The only bit left to do is the grove. Maybe the jigsaw puzzle will show us what the building in the middle is."

Boges had just arrived back at the house and came over to see, but I could tell that he had barely heard what I'd said. I understood. He could only focus on our caving mission and Oriana de la Force's next move.

"Right now," said Boges, "we've still got the upper hand. Oriana doesn't know how to get into the caves, but it's only a matter of time before

Curly figures it out. I've just had a look over the cliff and this bad weather is whipping up the swell, so I reckon we go for it tonight at the next high tide."

6:11 pm

The hours ticked down to the time for the high tide and the rain continued to pour down. Repro got up from working on the jigsaw puzzle and came over, sticking out his hands in front of the fire.

"Ryan," I said, "maybe you could lend Repro something he could swim in?"

"Um," said Repro. "About this night swim in the caves . . . "

"Don't tell me you don't swim?" I asked.

"Like a fish," he said. "But . . . "

"But what, Repro?" I asked. "I thought you'd jump at the chance to navigate through dark tunnels again."

He sighed. "I have to leave, or I'll be in big trouble with Correctional Services. I have to get the train back to the city. It leaves at 8:30."

"You can't possibly walk back into town in this weather," I said. "All your layers will get sodden."

"Winter," said Boges, passing over the keys to his truck, "Ryan and I can go get the metal box.

We don't need three people splashing around in there, and this rain is just going to make it miserable. If you drive Repro into town, you might be able to get Rose by herself. Anyway, we won't be leaving until after ten—high tide isn't till midnight," he continued. "It would be better if I set you up to monitor the live feed input from Skyshadow. If it looks like we're going to get some unwelcome company, you might have to warn us."

"How? You don't have underwater phones." For once, Boges didn't have an answer. "OK, OK," I said, taking the keys. "I get the feeling that Rose would love to help us—if she could. Come on, Repro. Grab your bag." I picked up my phone and some money, and pushed them into my back pocket.

7:13 pm

We set off through the rain, windshield wipers racing as I strained to see what was ahead of me on the road. Fortunately there wasn't anyone else around. We crawled along, fearing that we'd get stuck. I hoped that the rain was helping Harriet a little, but I was concerned about how Abercrombie House might stand up to this deluge, as I remembered the state of the roof.

It seemed to take ages to get into town. Eventually, we made it into the village and I dropped Repro off near the station under an awning. Rain poured off the edges and Repro danced to avoid the drips.

"Any other problems you might have," said Repro, "just let me know. I'll do what I can. Best of luck with solving the mystery. And by the way, I finished the jigsaw puzzle for you. My fingers just seemed to know which bits to put in."

"Fantastic, thanks! Bye, Repro," I said, and watched his lanky figure disappearing into the ticket office. From the doorway, he leaned out to wave to me one last time. I waved back, smiling.

I ducked into the shop, but Rose wasn't there. Instead, a young girl was behind the counter. "Wicked weather, isn't it?" she said. "And there's a cyclone system moving down the coast. You're just in time, we're about to close. What can I get you?"

"Cyclone? What do we do?" I asked, alarmed.

"We close everything up, batten down the hatches as they say. Tape up the windows and hope that they don't blow in. It's the flooding I worry about. But you should be safe up on Clifftop Drive."

"Oh, OK. I hope everything will be all right down here," I said. I was wondering whether swimming through the cave system was such a good idea now that the weather was getting worse. The slow drive into town meant I was running later than I'd expected. I was sure I'd be back before they set off. Just in case, I called Boges, but it went straight to voicemail. Ryan's phone did the same thing. I left a message, "Call me!" on both of them. I hoped that the caves' narrow entrance would protect them if they did go down there early. But I had a really bad feeling about it.

Outside the shop, the rain increased in intensity, whipped almost horizontal by the fierce wind. A couple of the locals, weathered fishermen in their oilskins, climbed into a car next to me. "Nasty storm. There's a king tide as well," I overheard the passenger say.

"People died in the last one back in 1962," said the driver, as the car took off.

I hesitated at the truck door. *Why did that date seem familiar?*

8:35 pm

Back in the truck, I drove as fast as I could. The weather was really shocking now. Whenever I caught glimpses of the sea through the trees, I was alarmed to see how huge the swells were, with dim waves breaking well before the shore. My concern about Harriet also grew. I'd have to make a quick check on her, to see if she was OK. She had no one else. The truck rattled and banged across the corrugated road. It kept sliding sickeningly as I braked at corners.

8:59 pm

I became aware of a vehicle coming up behind me, leaning on its horn and flashing its headlights. What was wrong? He was clearly trying to get my attention.

I drove on a little further, but the flashing headlights and the sound of the horn blaring through the rain made me think that maybe there was some big problem on the road.

I signaled and pulled over, waiting while the other vehicle drove up alongside. The driver wound down the window. Curly.

"You've got a flat tire at the back, young lady. You'll need a hand with that. Don't try and drive any further with it—you'll wreck the wheel."

Of all times to get a flat tire. I'd never changed a tire in my life. I jumped out of the truck as Curly got out of his car, and with my head down against the driving rain, I squelched around to the rear of the truck. I squinted at both back tires. I was turning to say, "They both look OK to me," when my arms were suddenly pinned behind me. "Hey! What do you think you're doing? Let me go!!" I struggled, my feet skidding on slippery mud.

"Take it easy, young lady, and you won't get hurt," Curly growled, strapping my wrists behind me with something that I couldn't see.

"Get off me! You can't kidnap people like this!" But he was already dragging me over to his car and shoving me in the back seat. My arms were twisted behind me, and before I could maneuver myself to try to unlock the back doors, he was behind the wheel and driving away.

"My boss just wants a little word with you," said Curly. "Now don't try anything, especially in weather like this. You don't want us slipping off the road and crashing over the cliff, do you? Shame you didn't fall for my little ghost trick and leave town." *I knew it!* It *was* Curly who'd tried to frighten me.

He was driving erratically, zigzagging from side to side on the muddy road, throwing me around in the back where I was helpless to save myself from being banged against the front seats or the door. I screamed, "Let me GO!" and strained as hard as I could against whatever was tying my wrists. I found it was just possible to grasp my phone. I needed to hide it before Curly realized I had it.

"If you want me to drive nicely, you have to behave, OK? Just calm down."

I could see there was no point in making a lot

of noise. There was no one to hear me. I calmed down and sat awkwardly back in the seat.

"Where are you taking me?"

"I already told you. The boss wants a word with you."

"You mean Oriana de la Force, don't you?"

Curly chuckled, and it wasn't a pleasant sound.

I craned my neck to try to see where we were heading when Curly suddenly swung off the road that ran from the town and headed up the rise towards the northern headland and the mansion. I knew I had to break free. My hands might be bound, but my legs weren't. I waited for my moment.

9:24 pm

The car braked with a jolt. Rain lashed our faces as Curly opened the door and pulled me out. I pretended to stumble backwards, falling awkwardly on my side, and pushed my phone under some bushes near the back stairs of the house.

"Come on, clumsy," he grumbled, and pulled me to my feet. He pushed me up a few steps and through the back door. Mud and water dripped from my jeans. Fierce growling terrified me, especially now that I had no hands to fend off any dog attack. But the Doberman was sitting, ears erect and ready to spring.

Curly hauled me past the living room and into

the room where Oriana de la Force sat. It was the first time I'd seen her since her appearance on television, furious about being arrested and about the cat's whiskers that had been drawn on her cheeks. Now, thinner and meaner looking than I last remembered, she glared at me, her penciled brows contracting in an angry frown under her spiky hair.

"Look what the storm blew in," she drawled. "Winter Frey. You didn't expect to see me again, did you?"

"What do you think you're doing?" I demanded. "This is kidnapping. It's a major crime. You'll be back in jail."

"I don't think so," Oriana said menacingly. "Curly, make sure she hasn't got a phone on her."

Roughly, Curly searched my pockets. "Nothing here, except some money."

"I'll put that away somewhere safe," smirked Oriana. Curly handed her the money. "Now, I want to know what you found in the secret passage."

"Some steps," I said, "going up into the third-story room at the front."

"Don't play smart with me, missy," said Oriana, springing from her chair and walking around to stand with her face thrust into mine. I nearly passed out from the stink of the strong perfume surrounding her. She prodded me hard in the chest. "You know exactly what I'm talking about. A famous sea captain lived in that house and he left . . . *indications* concerning the whereabouts of a certain shipwreck. Ring any bells?" I stared at her, playing dumb.

"It's no use lying. I know exactly what you and your friends are looking for. In fact, right now, your boyfriends are making preparations to go into the sea caves on the high tide. A friend of mine overheard some very helpful information being discussed at Perdita. We know about the metal box above the high tide mark and I'm pretty sure that in that box are the details of the Windraker's exact location."

A friend of hers! The spy who was listening at the window! I looked suspiciously at Curly.

"Your dumb friends are going to find it for me, and then I'm going to take it from them. I do love it when other people do the cold, dangerous, wet work for me." She chuckled in a very nasty way. "Even more dangerous than they know," she added.

"What do you mean?" I asked, now even more worried.

"They'll find out soon enough," Oriana sneered. On her desk, Oriana smoothed out a large sheet of paper. "I even have a complete diagram of Perdita. You've no idea how much information

I've gathered over the last few weeks." She pushed the diagram into my face as if she wanted to rub my nose in it, and as she did, I noticed something about the cellar. There was something on the floor . . . a mark that could have been a smudge, but I had a feeling it was something more. *If only I can get Oriana to keep talking*, I thought.

"If you know all that then," I said, "why have you kidnapped me?"

"To get you out of the way, my dear. I don't want any more interference." Oriana paused, but the gloating sneer shortly continued. "Your boyfriends don't know what I know. The Windraker went down with a cargo of 10,000 coins—gold coins—in mint condition. One came onto the market recently and do you know what it sold for? Over $4,000. That was for just one little coin. Can you do the math, little girl? When I find all 10,000, I'll be rich again. You destroyed my chances of recovering the Ormond Singularity. You will not ruin my plans this time."

She pushed her face right into mine, so that our noses were almost touching, and spoke with such hatred, drops of spittle seemed like venom dripping from her fangs. "You and your pathetic friends will never get in my way again. Those noisy cyclonic winds blowing outside have come on top of a king tide. That's when the sun, the moon and the earth are all lined up at high tide, increasing the gravitational pull. So what does that mean? The water is much, much higher than normal. This monster tide rises way above its usual level. Only happens once or twice in a century."

Fear gripped me, my blood ran icy. I thought of Ryan and Boges in that final cave with the high-water mark a few feet from the large cavern's roof. If the tide rose much higher, there would be no airspace left near the cave's ceiling. My friends would drown unless I got away in time to help them.

"This monster tide has a special name," Oriana sneered.

My body tensed up. I already knew the name of the monster tide! That torn piece of newspaper with the four words. It hadn't been a threat after all. There wasn't a serial killer in the city. Some-one had tried to warn us, and it wasn't Oriana. Someone had even told us how many days there were until the monster arrived.

"A group of people in 1962 were exploring the cave system and no one survived. The water flooded the town and even more people died. They'd forgotten how others had drowned fifty years before, when a similar combination of condi-tions collided. They'd forgotten the existence of—" her sneer twisted into a snarl "—the Drowner."

She turned to Curly. "Take her away and lock her up. Don't remove the wrist restraints!"

The screeching of a powerful car braking outside took everyone's attention. Someone came in through the front door. "Oriana! The waves have smashed some of the boulders out of the way," he called out. "Those kids will drown, and we'll be able to get in and get the box from their bodies as the tide goes down!"

Glistening in black all-weather gear, a tall man with close-cropped fair hair, and a tight, hard mouth in a gaunt face, lurched into the room. The dog wagged its tail and licked the water off the man's boots.

"What's this?" he said, jerking his head in my direction.

"Just a little stickybeak. You can deal with her later, Dragan."

I didn't like the thought of him dealing with me, and especially not the cold reference to my friends' lifeless bodies. I felt terrible despair as I was dragged roughly upstairs by Curly and thrown into a room with the door locked firmly behind me.

11:06 pm

Trapped in the room, my mind reeled as I tried to figure out what to do. Being kidnapped by

Curly—and everything Oriana had said, particularly about the Drowner, had left me in shock. And Dragan! His ruthlessness scared me. He must have been the one with the loud sports car. He'd been listening in on our conversations, lurking behind the curtain in Rose's shop. No wonder Rose was so frightened!

Now, Oriana, Curly and Dragan had all the information we had and even knew about the treasure on the shipwrecked Windraker. I thought of Boges and Ryan. I had to warn them about Dragan and Oriana, and about the building cyclone—the Drowner. If the cyclone surge had moved some of the heavy boulders near the caves' entrance, there would be no protection from the deadly sea. The boys could be smashed up against the walls of the sea caves and cut to pieces on the rocks!

As the minutes ticked by, I could feel my panic rising. I had to get away, but how? I had searched every corner of the room, but could see no way out.

Out the window I could see the semi-transparent roof of the wraparound verandah on the ground floor beneath. Rain pounded on it, making a terrible racket. But what did I think I was going to do? With my hands tied behind my back, I was helpless, useless.

I slumped against the wall, slipping down, my bound hands scraping painfully against the wall. My hands . . . it would be so much better if they were in front of me, instead of behind. I wondered if the TV shows were true, and that it was possible to step through the hoop formed by my bound wrists.

I got down on the floor and started trying the maneuver. I strained and heaved, stretching muscles I didn't know I had, pulling my joints painfully, powerfully driven by the terrible danger confronting my two friends. I concentrated every ounce of energy on pulling my bound wrists down under my bottom. Then, feeling like I was going to be completely squished, I folded one leg at the knee as tight as I could, until my knee was hitting my forehead and I couldn't breathe. I dragged the leg through the circle of my tied-up wrists. I repeated the same procedure, so much harder with my other leg taking up almost all the room. But finally, I unfolded my upper body and sat up straight, panting, aching all over. I'd done it! My hands were now in front of me. Even though they were bound, I could move my fingers and I was able to unlock the window. I used strength I didn't know I had left as I forced the window open, pushing it up with my whole body. I looked down again and gulped. There was no other way. I was going to have to jump and just hope that the verandah roof would break my fall and that the pounding rain would cover the sound of my escape.

OK, Winter, I told myself, *jump!*

Crash!

I smashed through the roof, but the tough material stretched a little before it tore under the weight of my body. I fell heavily onto the cement, violently wrenching my left ankle. The scream of pain didn't get past my gritted teeth and I rolled around on the hard surface, riding it out. For a few moments, all I knew was the awful pain and the noisy drumming of the rain.

When the agony subsided a little, I started wondering whether anyone had heard my fall. I needed to get away as quickly as possible. I attempted to stand. I stumbled immediately. *Oh no*, I thought. My left ankle won't hold me! What will I do? I have to get to Ryan and Boges! Holding on to the verandah railing, not caring that I was getting drenched, I hauled myself up.

I tested how much weight I could put onto my left leg. Only a tiny bit. I couldn't let that stop me. I pulled myself along the railing, arm over arm, until I was able to cautiously hop down some steps and onto the ground.

I hobbled around to the back of the house,

feeling around in the mud under the bushes for my phone. I seized it. Curly's car was still parked there. Praying it was open, I tried the door. *Yes!* I hoped that no one would hear the sound of the vehicle over this storm as I got in and started it up. Handicapped by my tied hands and afraid to turn on the headlights, I was barely able to see the road through the pouring rain as I coasted out, painstakingly slowly. I didn't know how soon Oriana's lackeys would realize I'd escaped and come after me.

The car slid and slipped on the muddy road, but I waited until I was a good distance from the house before I switched on the headlights so I could drive faster. It still took what seemed like forever to get near Perdita and the top of the cliff steps, where I skidded to a halt.

I looked in the rearview mirror. I could see a light shining in the distance behind me. Someone was coming after me!

Perdita

11:52 pm

Somehow, despite the darkness and the furious storm, and my injured ankle, I had to help Boges and Ryan before I was captured again by my pursuers. As I stumbled and slid down the treacherous steps, I imagined the water rising higher and higher, Boges and Ryan trying to keep their mouths and noses above the level of the rising tide. I imagined the ceiling of the cave only inches above their heads.

My left ankle had swollen up like a football. I was so slow, I could only go at a snail's pace. I felt a terrible howl unfold from the depths of my being as I realized there was no way I was going to be able to make it down the cliff to save my friends in time. I was helpless—worse, I was useless. There was no hope. I wondered how I would ever be able to tell Cal.

As I despaired, the light I had seen came towards me. Dragan was coming after me to "deal" with me. Filthy, injured and scared, I stumbled under an overhanging bush and hid.

The figure came closer, and I saw a kerosene lamp glowing. The yellow light reflected off Dragan's raincoat and the hat he held down against the wind. He looked up, searching. It wasn't Dragan! I scrambled painfully out from under the bush. "Harriet! Harriet!" I screamed. "Help me!"

"Winter? What are you doing out here?" she shouted. "And what are your friends up to? I was out looking for my chickens and I saw them heading for the beach! They shouldn't have gone down there—not in this weather. I yelled at them to stop, but they couldn't hear me. So I ran back to get a lamp. But we can't get down there now!"

The words flowed out of me in a torrent as I stumbled towards her. "Help me. My wrists! Please!" She caught my bound arms.

"Who did this to you?" she asked, cutting the nylon cuffs with a Swiss Army knife.

A tiny hope flickered in my mind as I remembered the map Oriana showed me. The mark in the cellar. It wasn't more than a hunch probably, but it was the only thing we had. If I was right, I now understood the strange rectangular rock carving near the cave's roof.

"Help me get back to Perdita!" I yelled. "I'll explain everything later. I've got to get down into the cellar. There might be a way to help the boys get out of the sea caves!"

"That's crazy!" said Harriet as she grabbed my arm and I leaned on her while we staggered to the house. "The sea caves would be a death trap right now! Please don't tell me that's where the boys were heading?"

"That's exactly where they are and there's a Drowner tide coming!" I shouted.

DAY 30

1 day to go . . .

12:01 am

We staggered into the hallway of Perdita.

"The cellar! It's through there—let's go!" I said, leaning on Harriet as we crossed the big front room. We grabbed a couple of Ryan's looped ropes that hung near the fireplace. I pressed hard against the acorn, waiting impatiently as the secret passage opened.

"So you found the passages," Harriet murmured. "I wondered if the rumors were true. But who tied you up?"

"A truly evil woman. I promise I'll tell you—" I froze in fear as outside, over the sound of the storm, came the roar of a powerful engine. "Oh no!" I cried. "Dragan!"

I looked around, trying to find a weapon of some sort, but it was too late. Harriet and I turned to face the intruder as his footsteps clumped down the hall. A masked figure pulled off a helmet. I could barely believe my eyes!

As fast as my limp allowed, I ran to him. "Cal! Cal!"

"I've been riding all night," he said. "I haven't even been home yet. I just knew something was wrong, Winter. I knew it when we spoke on the phone. You promised you'd tell me if something was going on here!"

I tried to describe what was happening as quickly as possible, knowing our friends' lives depended on it. "Cal, Oriana's in town, she has a thug coming after us and she's after the map to the shipwreck holding 10,000 gold coins. Boges and Ryan are in the sea caves looking for the map too—it's in a metal box tucked up at the top of one of the caves, but they don't know about the cyclone and the king tide. They're going to be smashed to pieces or drown down there, unless we can save them! And I think I know how. But you've got to trust me and we have to go down to the cellar right now."

Cal and Harriet stared, trying to comprehend what was going on. But I could see Cal understood there was no time for more explanations.

"Right," he said, following me into the secret passage. "No time to call the cavalry, then. Let's go get our boys! Oh, and it's nice to meet you, Harriet."

By the light of Harriet's lamp, we made our

way down the steps to the cellar. I ignored the pain in my ankle and pushed on as fast as I could, gasping under my breath at each throbbing step.

We rushed into the damp, stone room and as Harriet held the lantern up high, I looked around for a telltale mark on the floor. "If there's an opening into the sea cave through the stone floor, we might be able to help the boys!"

"Like another trapdoor?" Cal asked.

"We'll have to feel around for it. I just know it's here somewhere," I said. Our scrabbling fingers finally located two metal handles, and further digging revealed them to be attached to one particular flagstone. "Come on, Cal," I urged. "Help me lift this. You take this handle and I'll take the other."

"Got it, you ready?" Together, we slowly pried it open, while Harriet held the lamp over the opening to reveal heaving black water barely inches beneath the cellar floor. The terrifying roar of the angry sea filled the stone room.

"Oh my," Harriet breathed.

Cal and I looked at each other, but we couldn't let fear overtake us. We quickly looped one of Ryan's ropes over the iron hook, tightening it into a climber's knot, and pulled on it to make sure it was totally secure. "That should hold me," Cal said. "You two stay here and haul us up."

"Forget it," I said. "I'm coming too." I had no choice. I had to go down there, injured as I was. My friends' lives were on the line.

"You can't go down into that!" Cal yelled, above the growling ocean. He grabbed the rope from me. "No way, Winter."

But I insisted and payed out some slack, roping myself to him around my chest, securing it under my arms.

"You're injured," Harriet cried. "Let me go down there instead!"

"We need you up here, Harriet," I said, touched by her bravery. "You make sure the rope remains attached to the hook. You might have to haul us in and my ankle just can't take that strain. The water will buoy me up down there. I'll give three tugs when I'm ready, OK?"

I followed Cal, and put my head down into the hole in the floor, and immediately got a mouthful of saltwater as a wave broke over my face.

"Boges! Ryan!" I screamed at the top of my voice. Over the crashing roar of the sea sweeping through the sea caves, I thought I heard a feeble voice calling my name. A dim, elfin light glowed in the blackness as I searched, desperate to locate their whereabouts.

"Boges? Ryan? Where are you?"

"Over here! . . . air pocket . . . water . . . rising . . . "

"Where's Ryan?"

"Holding him . . . knocked unconscious . . . can't hold much longer . . . "

"Boges!" I screamed. "We're coming! Hang on!"

Cal jumped into the water and disappeared. The rope between us tautened. A glassy wave bulged up through the trapdoor, almost sucking me through the opening as I plunged into the freezing water, following in the direction I thought Cal had gone, trying to ignore the shock to my system. I swam out as strongly as I could with my one good leg, following the blurring light I could see on the other side of the cave.

"No! . . . " came the wailing voice.

"It's OK! We're roped!" I yelled, my head just above water, and scarily close to the roof of the cave.

12:12 am

It was the hardest swim of my life. The raging sea tried to take me down, swirling me around, pulling at my legs and throwing me hard against the walls of the cave. Bit by bit, swallowing water, my head occasionally bashing up against the ceiling of the cave, I just kept heading towards the light and Boges's voice.

It seemed a long time before a wave threw me against something soft.

"Cal! Winter! Thank goodness! Help me with Ryan! I'm losing him!" Boges screamed over the cacophony of the sea.

Cal grabbed Ryan's unconscious body and I managed to pull a big loop of the rope through the water, and wrapped it around him. As I did so, the huge waves smashed the jar that held the flashlight and we were plunged into complete darkness.

Groping around, I guided Boges's hand to the rope behind my shoulders. I felt him grab it. I had no idea which direction to swim in. So with Cal holding Ryan and me towing Boges, I gave three strong tugs on the rope with my grazed hands. Another wave smashed the four of us hard up against the roof of the cave and we were completely submerged. I was caught unaware, and was desperate to get a breath of air. My chest tightened, and I scrabbled at the roof to find an air pocket, but there was none. After all this effort, after finding the trapdoor and the boys, I was going to die in this dark, turgid water. But then, I felt the rope tighten and then a slow, strong pull. The water suddenly dropped and I breathed a choking sob of air. Harriet was hauling us in.

We were a heavy load and the sea was powerful, dragging us in the other direction. The water was almost completely at the top of the cave, and we could only breathe when the sea surged away, leaving a small air space near the roof, before gathering its strength to slam us up against the walls and roof of the cave yet again. I felt Boges swimming and kicking as hard as he could, helping to propel me along and I did the same to Cal, who had a harder job, trying to keep Ryan's face above the water.

Finally, my salt-stung eyes saw dim light and I realized we were close by the opening into the cellar near the roof of the cave. I saw Cal push Ryan ahead and a huge sea surge helped to wash them through the trapdoor. I tried to gain a handhold, but the stone edges crumbled away and another wave smacked the wind out of me. I frantically reached again, and with Boges hanging on tight behind me, another wave smashed us up and onto the cellar floor.

I fell in a gasping heap and looked up, blinking and exhausted into a bright light above me.

And found myself staring into the jaws of a snarling dog!

12:24 am

"What's going on?" I heard Cal say. My eyes focused on Oriana de la Force, Curly and Dragan, restraining the monstrous dog, while Oriana pointed a small silver pistol at us.

Harriet stood to the side of the iron hook, the rope she had been holding now in Oriana's other hand. Had she been playing for Oriana's team the whole time? What little strength I had ebbed out of me and I barely struggled to get up. All our efforts had been completely wasted. We were no match for this armed trio and I couldn't take my eyes off the silver weapon. The Doberman strained at his leash and Dragan looked as if he couldn't wait to let his beast rip into us.

But at least, I thought, Oriana wouldn't get her hands on the metal box.

I was wrong.

"How thoughtful," Oriana mocked, kicking Ryan's unconscious body. "The brave lad has held on to the prize despite everything!" It was true. I could see the top of the metal box fastened to Ryan's chest with bungee cords.

I heard Boges, sprawled on the floor nearby, exclaim in despair under his breath as Curly wrenched the box from Ryan and passed it to Oriana.

"Boges, the brain," jeered Oriana. "You thought you were smarter than me. Big mistake. Let's take a look at what we've got here," she continued, putting the small silver pistol away. "Winter, I told you I was going to win. You thought you could get away from me, stupid girl." She gave me a vicious kick to the ribs. I cried out in pain.

A massive wave crashed through the trap-door opening. The whole room trembled with the force, as water sprayed in like a geyser, hurling rocks onto the cellar floor.

Oriana, water swirling around her ankle boots, picked up one of the rocks and smashed the metal box. It fell apart. With a crow of triumph, Oriana seized the contents—a limp piece of fabric—and held it up to Curly's powerful flashlight. I saw her expression change from elation to rage.

"What's this? It's useless! It's all rotted! You kids—did you have something to do with this? Where's the real chart?"

I couldn't believe it. After all we'd been through—a bit of rotten vellum! No diagrams, no indications as to where the Windraker lay.

Wearily, Boges answered her. "That's the chart. It's been in a sea cave for over a hundred years. We didn't do anything to it."

That just enraged her further. We all got a good kick as she screamed, "Get up! You inter-fering little scumbags! You'll pay for this!"

"But it isn't their fault," said Harriet, stepping forward. "I don't know who you are but—" A slap across the face silenced her.

"I don't know who you are either, you little

witch, except that you're with this lot. Get up the steps now! All of you. Dragan, Curly, take them upstairs while I decide how to dispose of them!"

Another massive wave shook the cellar and a jet of seawater shot up through the opening in the stone floor, this time almost hitting the ceiling, showering water all over us. The cellar rumbled and groaned.

"Now! Get up there!" Oriana screamed, the silver pistol back in her hand. "I'm going to teach you all a lesson you'll never forget!"

We started shuffling towards the stairs. Harriet and Boges were ahead of Cal, who was supporting a now semiconscious Ryan. Dragan was behind us, his dog growling, ready to race up after us. I couldn't even think of escape, not with my sides bruised, my twisted ankle aching—I could barely walk. I slowly started up the stairs.

"Get a move on, Curly!" Oriana shrieked. "The water's rising!" I heard the *whoomp* of an enormous wave hitting the underside of the cellar floor, as the furious sea forced tons of water upwards.

Suddenly, there was a massive explosion and the walls of the passageway shook as if an earthquake had hit. I heard a bloodcurdling scream from behind us, suddenly cut short.

I spun around, but could see nothing in the darkness. Had Captain Greenlowe been storing explosives? I went down a couple of steps to peer back into the cellar.

I froze, stunned in my disbelief. The middle of the cellar floor had totally disintegrated. There was now only a gaping hole and the foaming, crashing waves! The last thing I saw as the Drowner sucked and pulled back towards the caves was Oriana de la Force's arms flailing helplessly as the churning water whirlpooled downwards into the cave. The Doberman was swimming crazily nearby. The iron hook rattled wildly with the rope still attached to it. There was no sign of Dragan or Curly at all.

"Run!!" I screamed up at the others. "The cellar's breaking up! The water's still coming!"

I grabbed on to Ryan and Cal, pushing them in front of me, ignoring the pain as we struggled desperately along the narrow passageway. Ryan stumbled, but Cal pulled him onwards. "We're nearly there, come on!"

Glancing back, I gasped as the raging sea lashed up behind me and flew up in my face. I couldn't let the Drowner take us now!

Epilogue

And so we survived the Drowner, and Perdita was still standing. No one knew if the Drowner had claimed any lives—but only Curly had been rescued, found clinging to a buoy halfway out of the bay. He'd have a lot of questions to answer with the police once he was discharged from the hospital. His wife, Rose, did not wait for his full recovery to pack her bags and leave. She came for a visit before she left.

"This is a beautiful old house," Rose said, "it's wonderful to see it full of life again." She sighed, then went on, "A month ago, I overheard my husband talking on the phone and he mentioned your name, and about how the Drowner would lead to Captain Greenlowe's treasure. I wanted to let you know what was going on here, but I was afraid of Curly and his new friends. I knew you were in danger. I found your address in his papers and scribbled the note on the old clipping of the last Drowner. I'm sorry, I hoped the clue would be enough."

I took her hand and squeezed it. "Thanks, Rose," I said. "I know you were only trying to help." My mind was finally at ease now that the countdown had ended.

In the following days, there were more surprises to come. The jigsaw that Repro had so expertly put together revealed another of Perdita's secrets. The puzzle was actually an enlargement of an old photograph of the house in its earlier glory. The building in the middle of the grove looked like some kind of elaborate marble construction, topped with a figure and a plaque. Could it be a grave?

Boges took a photo of the finished puzzle. He enlarged the image on the camera's screen, until we could just make out one of the words . . . *Perdita*.

Harriet gasped. "So she didn't run away. The dark version of the story must be true. She's still here."

A shiver of horror ran through me. I felt sad for what had happened back then, but also strangely relieved that the mystery was finally solved.

The very next day, Harriet spotted the sepia portrait of Perdita in my bedroom. "Why have you got a picture of my great-grandmother on your wall?" she asked.

"Your great-grandmother? No, that's Perdita Greenlowe, Captain Greenlowe's lost daughter."

"But I have exactly the same portrait upstairs in my bedroom. Right down to the pearl earrings."

When Harriet brought over the portrait of her great-grandmother, Blanche Abercrombie, and we placed it next to the photograph of Perdita Greenlowe, we could both see . . . *it was the same young woman!* Harriet and I looked at each other. "Look, I brought this, too. I found it just the other day as I was packing up the house."

Harriet showed me an old wooden jewelry box, containing a brooch and a hair comb, and also a piece of parchment.

When I opened it up, my eyes went wide. "Harriet, you're not going to believe this," I said, "but I think this is the title deed transfer showing Perdita Blanche Abercrombie left the Perdita house to her daughter—my grandmother, Ruby!"

"So if Perdita Greenlowe and Blanche Abercrombie *are* the same person—" I started to say before Harriet threw her arms around me.

"They *are!* They are! It means we're related. It means we both have family after all—each other!"

Tears sprang to my eyes. "So Daniel Abercrombie and Perdita Greenlowe did run away with each other. She must have started to use her middle name, Blanche. They married and had children!"

"And here we are," said Harriet, "a couple of

generations later. Winter, you don't know what it means to me."

"Oh, I do, I do!" I said, hugging her tight.

Cal and Boges stood smiling at us. I burst out laughing and crying all at once.

"I don't want to interrupt your family reunion," said Boges with a grin, "but this raises a very big question." I suddenly understood what he meant. "Who on earth is buried in the grove?"

Before I could say anything, Ryan burst back inside yelling. "Hey, guys! One of those huge cypress trees was uprooted by the cyclone. It's made a clearing almost right to the middle. We can get through now and see the grave!"

The tree had cut a swath through the tangle of the undergrowth and fallen across the once-white marble tomb, opening a wide crack across the top.

"Let's take a look inside the tomb. There might be a nameplate on the coffin," I said. "Maybe it's Captain Greenlowe who's buried here. Who's up for having a look inside?"

"I am," said Cal stepping forward.

"No, let me," said Ryan. Then we all pushed forward to peer through the crack.

"Huh? There's no coffin!" Harriet cried. "I knew it!"

Instead of a coffin there was a small, brick-lined room.

"Maybe he dug out a family vault?" I wondered. "Help me move this marble slab." We pushed the smaller half of the cracked marble lid out of the way, and looked more closely at the small chamber. As we watched, one of the bricks moved. Then it fell out. A trickle of water started behind it as more and more bricks crumbled. The falling tree had done more than just break the lid of the marble tomb, it had undermined the retaining wall of the underground room. Now the banked-up water was pouring out, but instead of filling the room, the water was disappearing like an underground river.

"That must be storm water," Boges said. "The grove must act as a huge drain."

"I hate to think of all that water just going to waste," said Harriet sadly.

"I don't get it, what's the point of this underground room?" Cal asked.

"It would have been a perfect place to hide a smuggler's booty," I said. "Who'd look under a tomb?"

"But he already had the cellar at the end of the secret passageway to hide goods in. This is weird."

"Well, he went to a lot of trouble to hide it," I said.

"And we know Perdita Greenlowe wasn't buried here in 1926," said Harriet, "because she married my great-grandfather, Daniel Abercrombie."

The final piece of the puzzle fell into place when we drove Harriet back to her house later that day. "What's that noise?" I asked.

"That sounds like water," said Harriet. "The culvert under the road must be overflowing."

Boges stopped the truck and we climbed out. An amazing sight met our eyes. Close to Abercrombie House, where the dried-out gully had been, a gushing river now flowed past the house, carrying swirling branches and leaves along with it as it raced past the fence line, towards the cliff.

Harriet stared in disbelief. "The river! It's started to run again!"

My mind jumped, linking two events—the

sudden flood under the fake tomb and the restored watercourse. Captain Greenlowe's curse on Abercrombie House suddenly made sense to me!

"Harriet! That's what the room under the tomb was for! Captain Greenlowe deliberately bricked up the watercourse so that it couldn't flow to Abercrombie House!"

Harriet blinked. "That's why our river dried up?"

"Yes," I said, nodding vigorously.

"He must have done that right after Perdita ran away with Daniel Abercrombie," Ryan said, "to destroy the Abercrombie family's property and punish the man who'd won his daughter's heart."

"But the river is running again. His curse is broken!" Harriet broke into a crazy dance. "I don't have to sell the farm!"

I felt Cal slip an arm around my waist. "After all these years, you two have brought the families together again."

Finally, I had not only my friends, but family too, my very own estate and nothing more to fear. Although I couldn't help but wonder if Oriana de la Force and Dragan might have survived the Drowner and been washed ashore somewhere. I forced myself to put her out of my mind once and for all.

It took a while to tell Cal everything that had happened and at first he was really angry with me for not having kept him in the loop. "You *promised*," he said.

"Cal, sometimes promises have to be broken. You needed to be at flight school, and we needed to figure out the mysteries here. Please try to understand."

Eventually he calmed down. "OK, OK," he said, "you're forgiven." Then he grinned. "You guys did do a pretty fantastic job. Between us, I think we could just about take on the world!"

33 11:45 RACE AGAINST TIME 06:48 07:12 05:21 RACE
E RACE AGAINST TIME SEEK THE TRUTH... CONSPIR
S TRUST NO ONE SOMETHING IS SERIOUSLY MESSED
30 12:01 05:07 06:06 06:07 MALICE WHO CAN WINTE
EK THE TRUTH 12:05 MALICE 06:04 10:08 RACE AGAI
27 08:06 10:32 SEEK THE TRUTH 01:00 07:57 SOME
RIOUSLY MESSED UP HERE 05:01 09:53 CONSPIRACY
CE AGAINST TIME 04:31 10:17 MALICE WHO CAN WINT
09 LET THE COUNTDOWN BEGIN MALICE HIDING SOM
32 01:47 05:03 MALICE LET THE COUNTDOWN BEGIN
IS RACE AGAINST TIME 06:48 07:12 05:21 RACE AGAI
CE AGAINST TIME SEEK THE TRUTH... CONSPIRACY
ONE 06:07 SOMETHING IS SERIOUSLY MESSED UP H
01 05:07 06:06 06:07 MALICE WHO CAN WINTER TRU
E TRUTH 12:05 MALICE 06:04 10:08 RACE AGAINST T
06 10:32 SEEK THE TRUTH 01:00 7:57 SOMETHING IS
SSED UP HERE 05:01 09:53 CONSPIRACY 365 12:00
HE 04:31 10:17 MALICE WHO CAN WINTER TRUST? 01:
UNTDOWN BEGIN MALICE HIDING SOMETHING? 03:32
LICE LET THE COUNTDOWN BEGIN, 09:06 10:33 11:45
HE 06:48 07:12 05:21 RACE AGAINST TIME RACE AGA
EK THE TRUTH... CONSPIRACY 365 TRUST NO ONE S
06:07 SERIOUSLY MESSED UP HERE 08:30 12:01 05:
07 MALICE WHO CAN WINTER TRUST? SEEK THE TR
LICE 06:04 10:08 RACE AGAINST TIME 02:27 08:06 1
E TRUTH 01:00 07:57 SOMETHING IS SERIOUSLY ME
RE 05:01 09:53 CONSPIRACY 365 12:00 RACE AGAINS
17 MALICE WHO CAN WINTER TRUST? 01:09 LET THE
GIN MALICE HIDING SOMETHING? 03:32 01:47 05:03
E COUNTDOWN BEGIN 09:06 10:33 11:45 RACE AGAINS
12 05:21 RACE AGAINST TIME RACE AGAINST TIME S
UTH... CONSPIRACY 365 TRUST NO ONE SOMETHING
RIOUSLY MESSED UP HERE 08:30 12:01 05:07 06:06
O CAN WINTER TRUST? SEEK THE TRUTH 12:05 MAL
08 RACE AGAINST TIME 02:27 08:06 10:32 SEEK THE